# POCKET DIAL

Sandy Magner

For Jimmy Blue Eyes.

# CHAPTER 1

How is it that I'm involved in this nightmare? At my age, you would think this shit was behind me. The police are telling me that I'm the only person who knows what happened to Tommy. Well, besides Dylan, that is.

Cell phones. Why did it have to be me that Dylan's cell dialed at that moment? Why am I involved with someone fifteen years younger than me? This makes me smile. I know why. He is tall, and tan, and has sparkly blue eyes and wavy blonde hair. All the makings of my grade-school crushes. I've lost ten pounds in three days. This pressure to tell the police what I heard is burning holes in my stomach. It's been three hours since they brought me into the police station. I'm hot, my armpits are soaked, and I've been shaking from my adrenaline rush since I opened the door to police officers on my front porch. My vision is blurred by multiple faces of snarling men. Over and over, they ask me what I heard. I feel paralyzed with fear. I've never been in trouble before. I know I should tell them what I heard when Dylan's cell dialed me, but I can't betray him. I need time to process. I need to talk to him. Maybe I heard it wrong.

He's such a sweet guy. Could I have heard it wrong? I feel so good when I'm with him. That's over if I tell them what I heard. Life was finally good because of Dylan. I'm not prepared to give that all up. Hell, it has only been three days since it happened. How can a good thing end this fast? Was it an accident? Or did he mean to kill that boy?

My brain feels like it's vibrating from all the noise in the room. The police are asking personal questions about my relationship with Dylan. I'm very uncomfortable. Does my ex-husband, John Goodwill, the town's mayor, have to be standing in the room frowning at me? All the babbling is making my ear's ring. I know I look like a pathetic middle-aged woman, protecting some young guy I've only known for five months.

"Ms. Burns, what is this guy to you? You know that Tommy was the son of one of our own, don't you? Tell us what you heard!" seethes one red-faced cop.

I feel like I've been captured by the enemy. How do they know I heard something? Did I say I heard something? I look from one cop to the other and then to my ex-husband. I know he was called in to help convince me to come clean. I'm still close with John, though we've been divorced for nearly ten years. Since we had produced two great kids together, there's a level of respect and support we have for each other. John steps in at one point when the yelling from the police is becoming abusive towards me. He tells the officers to back off and let me go home. John is also a lawyer, which helps him be more persuasive.

One officer sits so close to me, I can feel the hair from his arm. He moves closer and whispers to me, "If you don't tell us what you heard, you'll be going to jail for obstruction. Think about that when you're home."

His face is a few inches from mine, "Do you hear me, Jen Burns?"

I look up at him and say, "Yes. Can I go home now?"

The officer nods yes and extends his hand to me. I reject it and slowly peel myself up from the chair I've been glued to for the last three hours. I look behind me to see sweat marks on the seat. *Oh, god!*

Pushing open the front door of the police station, my knees buckle. I hold on tight to the door's handle, and John grabs my arm from behind. He whispers into my ear, "Some mess you've gotten yourself into, Jen."

John holds my arm until I get into my car, and then follows me home. When I get into the driveway, it takes me a moment to get out of the car. I can feel John watching me. My body is weak, but I get myself to the front door. I lock the door without looking back at John. I don't want to talk to him right now. I'm hysterical, embarrassed, and sad.

I climb into the "queen's chair," named by my kids. It's where I used to spend most nights in front of the TV before Dylan came along. While pulling up the plaid throw onto my lap, I put my head back and try to get the noise out of my head. As I warm up, I let myself remember when I met Dylan. It was a Tuesday. My favorite bar. I was there with my partner-in-crime, Katrina. "Class Clown, class of '85!" is how I always introduce her. She can make anything funny. Nothing is out of bounds for Kat. Most of her skits contain jokes about our being old and single. She's been my friend since we were six years old. When I was in school, I felt lucky that the funniest and most popular girl was my best friend. She is as loyal as my dog, never judging me and always making me laugh at myself.

We started the evening at the Barnacle Bill's bar with the usual banter about how pathetic our lives are; me for being divorced two times and her for never being married at all. It only took me two seconds to notice the hottie sitting one seat away.

I said to Kat, "Do you see that?" with a tilt of the head in his direction.

Kat pushed a strand of unruly, curly brown hair behind her ear and said, "Duh!" Then she paused and said, "Too young, like twelve!"

I lifted one brow and said, "Maybe for you, not me!"

Two drinks later, I was leaning over to ask boy-hottie how old he was and if he dates older women. At first, I did it to make Kat laugh, but when he turned to answer me, he smiled and said, "Thirty, and sure."

I heard Kat behind me say, "Oh, here she goes!"

My new friend was charming and sweet. He reminded me of the actor, Paul Walker, from *The Fast and The Furious* film series. He was tan and blond, with pretty blue eyes. My body temperature jumped ten degrees. I thought he was kidding. He had to be messing around with us, two old ladies at the bar. But he seemed genuine. I couldn't tell if he meant, "Sure, I'll date you," or "Sure, I date older women."

Kat knew by my sudden silence that my liquid courage must have been wearing off.

She fluttered her eyelids over her greenish-brown eyes while she leaned over towards the guy. "Well, my friend here thinks you're cute and wants to go out with you. What do you think?"

With that, I felt like an idiot. Why would a guy like him want to go out with me? I was in pretty good shape for my age and my hair was still light blonde, but still. As Kat loved to say, "You ain't no supermodel!"

For the next hour, we sat at the bar, talking and laughing. I found out his name was Dylan Jagger. I remember feeling skittish by how intensely he looked at me when I spoke. Was he really interested? When we got up to leave, he asked me for my cell number. As I rambled out the number, he put it directly into his cell phone and gestured, "Saved!" He winked and said he'd be in touch.

Kat and I giggled all the way to the car.

Kat pestered me, "What's wrong with you? He's way too young for you!"

"Oh, who cares? Let me have some fun! He probably won't call me anyway, so chill!"

I remember getting home and feeling high from the attention, which wasn't something I had felt in a long while, since my second divorce. Yes, I tried it twice. The first marriage was for his love. The second marriage wasn't. Both marriages had failed for good reasons, but that didn't make me feel any better about being a "two-time loser." I hopped into bed and was about to fall asleep when my phone rang. I didn't know the number. I picked it up and said,

"Hello?" It was Dylan! Oh, my God, it was Dylan!

He said, "Can we get together soon?"

I stumbled over my words, but what came out was, "Sure!" Just the way he had said it earlier that evening. I clicked "end" on my phone, reopened my cell, and added Dylan to my contact list.

My stroll down memory lane is interrupted by a hammering on my front door. I jump from my chair and peer out the front window. Was it more cops? Was it John, back to yell at me? I see Brandy, Kat's dog, sniffing around the front yard.

"Hey, dumbass. You in there?" Kat yells.

I slowly unlock the door with my head pressed up against it, and open it to see an annoyed look on Kat's face.

"What's wrong with you? Just tell them what you heard, and send the asshole to jail!"

I lower my head and walk into the kitchen.

"I can't," I say softly. "I need to speak with him. I can't betray him." My eyes are welling up with tears, and that softens Kat a little.

"Okay, tell me what you heard."

We sit down in the kitchen. I pick up my cell, mimicking how I picked up my phone, and explain what happened three days ago.

"It was about 4 p.m. on Wednesday. I was up in my bedroom putting away laundry, when my cell phone rang. It was Dylan again. I let it ring an extra time. I had just spoken to him, while he was on the way to his friend Pete's house. I answered, 'Miss me, huh?' No reply. I thought he must have pocket dialed me, and was about to hang up the phone, when I heard Dylan's voice. It was muffled a little, but I could hear him talking to Pete's son Tommy. They were giggling and talking loudly, so I kept listening."

I'm embarrassed, admitting this to Kat.

"I was a little nervous that Dylan might catch me eavesdropping, but I couldn't stop listening."

Kat's right eyebrow rises a bit and she shoots me a disapproving look.

"I was about to hang up when I heard a light cry. Like a baby crying. I waited on the phone to hear more. I could hear a muffled voice say, 'Stop, Dylan! That hurts.'"

I put my hands in my hair and say, "Kat, my heart started pounding out of my chest. I was wondering what the hell Dylan was doing to this kid to make him say that. Then Dylan says back, 'You think that hurts, Tommy? How about this?'"

I grab a pillow off the couch and put my face into it and tell Kat that Tommy's cries sounded muffled, like this. I even think Dylan might have been sitting on him.

Kat looks puzzled. "You can't be right; Dylan seems like such a nice guy." I agreed with Kat, but then I tell her more.

"I heard Dylan say Tommy's name over and over again, all creepy-like. Teasing him and making him cry even harder."

I try to mimic Dylan's voice and say, "How about this, Tommy? Does this hurt? Are you scared now, Tommy?"

I tell Kat that I heard more muffled cries. "Then there was nothing. Silence. It seemed like forever. I felt like I couldn't breathe. I didn't know what to do. I thought, *Should I hang up and call the police, or keep listening?* I tried to convince myself that it was all a gag. It seemed like ten minutes before I heard a new voice. It was Pete's voice, Tommy's dad. I felt relieved that he was there. I thought maybe everything was going to be okay. I felt stupid for getting worried. But, Kat, it got worse."

I continue to mimic the voices of those I heard.

"'What's wrong with Tommy? Why is he blue?'" I yell, trying to mimic Pete's voice, then look at Kat. "I nearly died when I heard him ask Dylan that. Dylan answered, 'I don't know. I just got here and found him this way.'"

In Pete's voice, I say, "Where's Christine? Shouldn't she be watching him?"

I interrupt myself, gesturing to Kat with my hands extended. "What? Why would Tommy be alone without a babysitter?"

"Then I heard a lot of frantic yells to call 911, and someone yelling, 'Tommy isn't breathing.'"

Looking at Kat, I start to cry, feeling the same panic I felt that afternoon. With my hands in the air, I shout out, "I should have done something, Kat! I should have stopped him. I should have yelled to him to stop."

Kat steps up from the table and says, "I don't know what I would have done or what I'd do now. How much do you like this guy? Is it worth it? Is *he* worth it?"

In between sobs, I question myself. "I don't know."

We sit down in silence. After what seems like an hour, I say, "Remember how hot my first date with Dylan was?"

Kat smirks. "Yes, you cougar."

We laugh.

It was two days after I met Dylan that he called and asked me to meet him at this public bar located in the basement of someone's house. I'd been there once before, so I knew where it was. I got Kat and her boyfriend of eight years, Scott, to meet me there. Dylan was a bartender at a bar not too far from there, and said he could meet me at about 9 p.m., after he got off. "Excited" would be an understatement of how I felt getting ready that night. I was all primped, trimmed, shaved, and plucked. I was ready for anything.

Kat, Scott, and I were there on time. I quickly got my drink of choice, orange vodka and club soda, and sucked it down. I was really nervous, almost panicked. I kept thinking to myself, *What am I doing? He won't show!*

Dylan walked in with his work T-shirt on. Normally it would have bothered me that he hadn't changed, but this time, I let it slide. He walked right up, wrapped his arm around my waist, and kissed me right on the lips. I hadn't expected such confidence from him this early on. It felt awkward in front of my friends, but secretly I liked it. That sort of broke the ice for me.

He said hello to Kat, and she shot back with, "Hey, do I get one of those kisses?"

Laughing, he said, "Sure, if you want!"

He leaned in, and I smacked him back. "No way, Kat, he's mine!"

The night flew by. I felt comfortable with him. It was like we'd been dating for months. We had great chemistry. He kept kissing my face. At one point, Kat asked him to kiss me again so she could get a picture with her cell phone. He made me feel sexy. He told me how pretty he thought I was. I was loving life. I remember him saying something about how he only dated really pretty girls. Somehow that didn't sit well with me, but my ego loved it.

We all left the bar around 1 a.m. Dylan walked me to my car, and I asked if he wanted to come back to my house. I didn't want the night to end. I knew we could hang out longer because my kids were at their dad's house. I was naïve to think that that was all we'd do. We got in my car and drove to my house, with him flirting and teasing me the whole way.

Once we got to my driveway, he didn't hesitate. Leaning over, he grabbed my face between his hands and kissed me. I kissed him back, my heart racing. After what seemed like ages, I realized that the neighbors might be watching us, and pulled away. I grabbed his arm and said, "Let's take this inside."

Inside, Dylan looked around. "Nice crib."

I guided him into the living room. I turned on the flat screen TV as I lowered myself into the queen's chair, but had barely taken my seat before he was kissing, touching, and grabbing all over me. I remember thinking that I should stop this, but it had been a long time since my last relationship, and I wanted it. I felt his fingers at my belt buckle, and then *swish*, off went my jeans. He kneeled in front of me and took me in, grabbing my lower butt and pulling me towards his mouth. I was surprised that I felt no awkwardness—not something I usually favored. I was always embarrassed by oral.

He used his tongue to lick and plunge into me, getting me so excited that it didn't take me long to go over the top. My body jolted and trembled, and he rose to his feet and leaned in to kiss me.

"It was nice to meet you," he whispered.

That was it?

We dressed, and he left. He said he was walking to his friend Pete's house, where he said he stayed often. Later, I found out that Dylan's parents had died within a year of each other, and that he hadn't really found a place to live yet.

Kat and I sit a while longer, debating over what I should do. I tell her that I want to find out more about the legal end of this, and that the police had told me Dylan was being charged with manslaughter for killing little Tommy. During my interrogation, the police officers kept reiterating what a bad guy Dylan was for killing his friend's son. The police said that Tommy was asphyxiated, that it had been roughhousing that got out of hand. They said the pillow was wet, which they thought was from Tommy's tears, or even worse, his spit. They're waiting on DNA results. They said that this pretty boy, Dylan, was a mean kid with a history, that I shouldn't be protecting him, and that I was going to go to jail myself.

I grab Kat's arm. "What do you think they are talking about with 'his bad history?' Would I really get in trouble for not telling the police what I heard that day? What would happen to Dylan if I did? What evidence did the police have to arrest Dylan for manslaughter? I need to call John to find out more of the details."

Kat rolls her eyes. "Good luck with that!" She says, her voice scratchy.

# CHAPTER 2

I'm trying to wrap my head around this killing-a-kid thing.
This can't be real. This Dylan is not my Dylan. The man who kisses
me so gently. The man who proudly holds my hand when we walk in
public. The man who is always attentive to my needs. He goes out of
his way to help me with anything. If I'm running late, he suggests
that he can pick up my kids, Lauren and Jack, from the high school.
He even walks the dog.

Physically, he's a beautiful man. I love to just sit and look at
him. When he catches me staring, he says nothing and smiles. His
skin is tan and smooth, and his long eyelashes frame his blue eyes.
His body is lean and fit and his ass is *perfect*. He wears old Levi's
like he was born in them. He stands six feet tall and never slouches.
He is like a piece of precious art to me. How did I get this lucky?

I love when he draws me in closer when we kiss. Oh, God,
those nights of amazing sex! He is uninhibited and in tune to what I
want, what I need. He tosses me around like I'm as light as a feather.
He likes to be the dominator. I love knowing that he desires my

body. After sex, he rubs my back and tells me how beautiful I am. I was even just starting to like it when he grabs my neck and squeezes, just enough for me to get a head rush, making intercourse even more titillating.

He also shows such concern for my well-being. I got a terrible cold a few months back, and he came to my rescue, making chicken soup and going to the pharmacy for me. I never need to ask him more than once to move a car, or even to bring the garbage pail to the curb. He never seems mad or upset with me. He kisses my face all the time. He laughs at my stupid jokes. He even seems to like Kat's sarcasm. How can this man be the same man I heard on the phone terrorizing a young boy? This must all be a bad joke.

Out of all the men I have ever dated, Dylan was the first man who actually listens to me when I speak. I can be very intense when telling a story, but he has never shied away. He's always ready with a pertinent question. He's supportive when I'm upset, and never diminishes my feelings. Even when he disagrees with me, he does it with a smile.

Admittedly, we haven't been as close since I asked him to move out, but this is unfathomable. Can he really be this black-and-white? A lovely human being one minute, and a murdering monster the next? How can this be true? I wish I'd never picked up his call. I can't undo hearing the anger and disdain in his voice towards an innocent child. What had Tommy ever done to him?

I feel sorry for myself. I know the wonderful times I've had with Dylan are now tarnished. He isn't beautiful and shiny anymore. I know I can't love a man who would do this to a child. My brain is telling me my fantasy love affair is over, but my heart isn't ready to let him go.

# CHAPTER 3

I haven't heard from Dylan since he pocket-dialed me. I was told that he was being held at the police station in Tree Lawn Township. This isn't surprising, since he's being accused of killing his friend Pete's son, and Pete Butler has been a police officer in my one-square-mile town, Tree Lawn, for twenty years. He's a big, tall guy that everyone likes, and he has an open-door policy at his house. Need a helping hand, and Pete is there. Even when he's off-duty, you'll find him helping a neighbor move or build a deck. That's how Dylan came to know him and his family. He found himself on Pete's couch many nights after bartending until 2 a.m. Pete's house seems to have a revolving door for friends (and, rumor has it, women).

Pete had three children from three separate women. Tommy was the offspring of his most recent love interest. Every time I saw Big Pete, he would give me a toothy smile and open his arms for a bear hug. I loved getting those bear hugs. He was non-judgmental and could keep a secret. He had helped me one night when I couldn't get my second husband, David, off the front lawn after another night of drinking too much. He was driving by in his patrol car and stopped when he saw that I was having trouble getting him into the house. Pete helped me without any unwanted advice or lectures. Actually, now that I think of it, he never mentioned it to me again.

I met my second husband, David, through work. I'd been single for five years when we met. I think my standards had waned because I was lonely. I was working for a mutual fund company, and he as a fund manager. He was wealthy and had been married for twenty-five years. I worked for Manhattan Mutual Funds as an assistant to three of the sales agents. We met when we both attended one of the big MMF conferences down in Atlantic City, New Jersey. I was in charge of all the arrangements for the conference, and David was one of the guest speakers.

David was short in stature but tall in ego. He was rich. I knew that he made millions managing one of MMF's most popular mutual funds. He was one of several VIPs that I had scheduled a flight from Manhattan to AC by helicopter for. Since I was in charge of the conference, I was very busy, being pulled in many directions. I hadn't noticed David when he arrived to the conference room because he had flown in with the company's CEO, Mike Pierson. I was very concerned about impressing Mr. Pierson, so I thought nothing of David when he came up to introduce himself to me. David was somewhere between average-looking and handsome. He had a very endearing smile, and stared right into my eyes when he asked how the set-up for the conference was going. He surprised me by giving me so much attention. He listened intently to my answers to his questions. This made me notice him more. He had all eyes on me during the conference. Any time I caught him looking, he would smile warmly. He made me feel proud of the job I was doing. At first, I really didn't think there was more to it. But I was wrong. David, I would soon find out, was in hot pursuit.

After David presented his speech, he walked off the stage and came directly up to me. He asked, "What did you think of my presentation?"

I was thrown by the question. I was just an administrative assistant. I was in no place to tell him what I thought of his presentation. I felt my face flush. I decided that if he was going to ask, I was going to answer. "It was a little boring, like one big run-on sentence. Your voice was also a bit too monotone." When I looked up from the floor his mouth was hanging open, but he was smiling.

He laughed. "Wow. You really think so, huh? You know, no one's ever said anything like that to me before. I like that about you! The fact that you're a tall, pretty blonde with beautiful, big brown eyes helps also."

For the rest of that conference, he kept returning to me for idle chatter, even once drinking from my water bottle. I never knew that his intentions were much more than an innocent flirtation until a week later, when I received an email from him asking me to look over one of his presentations. I thought, *This guy is brilliant. Why is he asking me what I think?* The funny thing was, when he sent me his presentation, it was one long, run-on sentence. At first, I thought he did it on purpose to be funny, but after emailing back my rewrite with bullet points and some suggestions he replied with just a 'thank you.' No caps, nothing else.

For months after the conference, he continued to call and

email me. I was flattered by his attention. At some point, he asked me to meet him in the city. I knew he was married, but at this point, I was infatuated with him.

I took a ferry into the city, and he was waiting at the pier for me in his convertible Lexus. When he saw me, he jumped from his seat and ran to open the passenger door for me. He was acting like such a gentleman. The restaurant he took me to was sleek and modern. The food was delicious, and the conversation was fluid and fun. It was perfect. I was feeling tipsy when we left the restaurant. He held my hand and whispered, "Do you want to go to a hotel with me?" I knew I should be a *good girl* and say 'no thank you,' but at this point, I was blindly smitten.

These dinner dates became a bi-weekly ritual. We thought that these trysts would be enough for us, but we were wrong. We fell in love. Or at least, I thought it was love.

David liked to spend money on everything from booze to cars. He often presented me with expensive jewelry. I was living a fantasy life with him.

After a year, the relationship had become all-consuming. I was tired of being with someone married and unavailable. I wanted out, but David wouldn't hear of it. He pursued me even more by trying to control where I went and what I did. He promised to leave his wife so that we could be together. I was enamored with him, so I trusted him. He got divorced. He angered many friends and family members, and it cost him more than half his net worth.

A year later, we got married, but didn't live happily ever after. I believe that we never had a chance because our union began as a shady affair. We lived together under a dark cloud of others' resentment and pain. This was not a marriage based on honesty.

Two months into the marriage, karma kicked me in the ass. I caught David having an affair with his old high school girlfriend.

He had blamed it on his drinking problem and pleaded for my forgiveness. Even though my love for him was marred, I stayed with him for a few more years. Soon after he got 'out of control' with his spending and his drinking, I planned an escape. When I got financially more secure I would leave him. We divorced after four turbulent years, and I haven't spoken to him since.

# CHAPTER 4

Kat and I sit in silence at the kitchen table for what seems like days, until Kat starts talking to her dog, Brandy, and my golden retriever, Riley, who she's nicknamed "Coyote." Kat has an unusual relationship with her dog. It's as if Brandy speaks back to her. She rescued Brandy from living in a tree near her family's greenhouse. When she speaks to Brandy, she answers herself in a funny, deep voice.

Kat had just asked Brandy, "What should Jennifer do about this man who killed a kid?"

She answers herself in Brandy's voice, "Did he at least eat him after?"

I jump up. "Not funny, Kat!"

Kat answers again for Brandy, "You humans are too sensitive!"

Brandy turns and walks away. Kat has irritated her with her bad humor. I can't help laughing at Kat. Leave it to her to make fun of even the worst of situations. Suddenly, we stop laughing, and sit in silence. I look at her, and she shakes her head back and forth.

Coughing, she says, "Jen, I don't know what I would do. No,

that isn't true; I would turn his ass in even if the sex *is* great!"

This makes us laugh again. Suddenly, the dogs run to the front window of the house, barking and making a big ruckus. Riley wags her tail when she sees who it is. It must be someone she knows. I open the front door to see John standing there in his navy pinstriped suit. He is sulking, an expression he wears often, so it doesn't alarm me.

Once John steps in the door, Kat gets up out of her chair and flies by us, saying, "I'll call you soon. Hang in there."

With a wave of her hand, she reluctantly says, "Hey, John."

Out the door she goes, with Brandy at her heel. John shakes his head like, *Oh well, your loss*. John and Kat never really saw eye-to-eye; John is a staunch Republican, while Kat, being liberal, is what she thinks is the underdog middle class. Although, Kat will be the first to say that John is very good-looking. He's the definition of "tall, dark, and handsome." I met him when I was twenty-three years old, and fell for him fast. We met at a bar in a nearby beach town one late night. We were engaged two months later. My dad said that he was the "marrying kind." His most attractive feature is how smart he is. He really knows his stuff. He knows a lot about American history and American law. John was in law school when we met, so we got married the summer after he graduated. He ended up being a great friend and a great father, but the chemistry between us faded after eight years of marriage. It was my insatiable need for romance that ended our marriage.

John walks past me and sits at the kitchen table. John and I had built this house together twelve years ago. It's a two-story colonial with a white picket fence. We had all the makings of the "American Dream." We designed the kitchen to open up into the living room. The kitchen table is the centerpiece of the house, and where everyone spends most of their time.

He opens a file on the table and starts to speak to me in his "lawyer voice." I feel my stomach turn. Quietly, I sit at the other end of the table.

In his deep voice, John starts, "Dylan is being charged with reckless manslaughter. That's the unlawful killing of another human while being reckless. The police are saying that there are extenuating circumstances; that Dylan knew that placing a pillow over Tommy's face could result in his death. They think he simultaneously smothered him with a pillow and compressed his torso by sitting on him. He could get up to twelve years in prison."

I lean in. "Did Dylan tell the police that he did that?"

John looks at me, annoyed, and says, "I shouldn't be telling you any of this, but no, Dylan has stated from the beginning that he found Tommy like that. That he had gotten to the house right before Pete came home." John takes a deep breath and continues, "They also found fresh scratches on Dylan's forearms."

I interrupt and ask, "Has there been an autopsy?"

"They're doing one now. No results yet," he replies, still looking down at the papers in front of him.

His eyes dart up from his papers, which startles me. In a deeper voice, he exclaims, "You'll be charged with obstruction of justice and end up in jail if you don't tell the police what you heard."

As John says this, I hear one of our kids open the door to

their room upstairs. Neither Lauren nor Jack have said much to me about what has happened. I'm sure that Facebook has been full of details, both true and false, since it happened. "Small-town police officer's son found dead." I want to sit down with them to talk about it, but haven't found time since it happened. I haven't even told my parents yet. I knew what they would say to me. Pretty much what John has just said.

I sheepishly ask, "When will Dylan get out of jail?"

He looks down in disgust. "Bail hearing is set for Monday morning."

John raises his head and looks at me with an expression I've only seen once before, the day we stood in a courtroom to get divorced nine years ago. He seems sad, but mad at me at the same time. He knows I just got divorced for the second time, and that I was having a hard time being alone again until I met Dylan. He mentioned to me a few weeks ago that I seemed to be doing way better.

John has a soft spot for me, so I'm surprised when he yells, "Tell them what you heard! Dylan is a freeloading asshole who has been taking advantage of you and this house. Think of our kids! Stop being so damn selfish! A five-year-old kid is *dead* because of him!"

The intensity of his voice pushes me back in my chair. I know what he's referring to, but I don't totally agree with him. Soon after I had that first date with Dylan, he broke his kneecap. He had done this to himself one night after drinking too much with his buddies. They went swimming in a random pool. It was dark, and he was drunk, and when he went to jump off a diving board, he lost his footing and landed on his kneecap. He called me the next day from Pete's couch, and told me he had shattered his knee and had to have reconstructive surgery. I told him that I had had a similar surgery to my right knee five years ago, and that the first few days post-surgery would be very painful.

Even though we had only known each other for a short period of time, I insisted he let me take care of him in my house for the week following his surgery. That one week turned into two months. To John, he was a freeloading asshole. To me, he was my saving grace. I did ask Dylan to move out once he got into a hard cast, but not for my lack of affection for him. I had grown uncomfortable with what others were saying. Neither my parents nor John had approved of these living arrangements, with my kids in the house.

I look right at John, but say nothing.

John jumps up from the chair and says, "I can't deal with you like this. Get some sleep, and we'll talk more about it tomorrow." With that, he walks out the front door. Riley follows, but he pays her no mind. He's pissed.

Since it's Saturday, I'm hoping to get a break from all of these questions and just have time to think about everything. Hopefully, I'll feel calmer and will call my parents. They won't have heard what happened because they live down in Florida. Luckily for me, they aren't on any of the social media sites. They're *New York Times* purists, and this small-town murder hasn't reached that stature.

# CHAPTER 5

It's 7:30 p.m. on Saturday. I can't remember the last time I sat down to eat something. Luckily for me, my kids are teenagers and self-sufficient. The last three days were such a blur. It was like I was watching this happen to someone else. I feel sad and lonely again. I miss Dylan. We used to keep in touch all day, every day, by text or calls. He is—or was—a very attentive boyfriend. The time that Dylan and I spent together while he lay helpless on my couch had created a deep connection between us, or so I thought. We would talk into the night about life and our past relationships. John had expressed concern for the safety of our kids after he had stopped by the house to find Dylan on the couch with his leg up. I had convinced him that even if Dylan were a serial killer, the soft cast on his leg wouldn't allow him to move very fast. He had nodded yes. I had calmed his fears. But now I wondered: had I put my kids in some serious danger?

One late night, Dylan had told me that both his parents had died within five years of each other. He still had a stepfather living in a house near the beach, but didn't like to go there much now, with his mother being gone. His father had died of a sudden heart attack a year before his mother. His mother was taking the garbage out one cold night and slipped on the slick driveway. The coroner had told him, his brother, and his stepfather that she had died instantly.

During the time he stayed here, we were more friends than lovers. That was okay with me, because I loved to take care of someone who really needed me. Plus, he was *cute*. My kids had stopped needing me 24/7 years ago, so it was fun for me to play nurse for a few weeks. He looked like a sweet child in the morning, with his hair all messy. Every day, he would say how much he appreciated what I was doing for him. Little did he know that I was happy to help him, because it guaranteed that I would see him every day. Two weeks after his surgery, Kat accused me of being like that crazy woman in the movie *Misery*, where she breaks the author's legs to keep him captive. When she said that to me, I had to think twice about whether she was right. She got me to do that a lot with her raw humor: pause and think about whether there was some truth to her joke.

At night, after making dinner for Dylan and the kids, I would snuggle up next to him on the couch. He would rub my calves, my hands, and my back. He told me how pretty he thought my face was. When you're forty-five, "pretty" doesn't come to mind. "Attractive," maybe, but "pretty" was a word used to describe those who were in their twenties. I would tell him he was crazy and blind. His rebuttal was always the same: that he only dates pretty women. He had said this a few times during those months. I crave to hear it now.

Every few days, he needed to bathe. Getting him up the stairs to take a shower was difficult. He would have to sit on the stairs and drag himself up, since the temporary cast was stiff and kept his leg straight. He couldn't bend his knee at all. He endured a lot of pain while he climbed the stairs. He would often wince. This is when I played the part of "mom." I had to baby him and encourage him to keep going. I needed to undress him, which I enjoyed. I loved to see his chiseled abs. Then I would sit outside the shower, waiting to see if he needed help. I started to love Dylan during this time. The relationship wasn't normal by any regards, but it was working for me.

The day I told Dylan that he needed to find somewhere else to convalesce was a sad one for me. I wasn't sure if that would be the end to our sexual relationship. Kat and my parents had convinced me that Dylan and I needed to date, not live together. My parents were annoyed that he hadn't contributed any money since he had (temporarily) moved in. They worried that I was being taken advantage of. I was tired of hearing about it, but also agreed with them a little. I wanted to see if Dylan would still hang around me once I wasn't his nursemaid. I was taking a chance that I would never see him again, but I needed to know if it was really me he liked. During his stay, he never referred to me as his girlfriend. I figured I was too old to have to hear him say it.

Now I was protecting him like his mother, not his girlfriend. I wish he had told me, even once, that he loved me. We were dating, yes, but he never committed to more than that. When I think about the fact that I'm fifteen years older than him and have two teenage children, I feel pathetic. I wish I could snap out of this infatuation. I know that that's all it is.

# CHAPTER 6

It's Sunday morning. I wake up to Riley scratching my bedroom door. I look at the clock and am amazed that it's 8 a.m. I never sleep past 6 a.m. I walk past Riley and down the stairs. It's quiet. I have until eleven before the kids get up. I make coffee and sit at the kitchen table with my cell phone in front of me. I stare at this new phone that my best friend from college, Ally, insisted I buy. *Fancy-ass, good-for-nothing phone.* I laugh to myself for blaming my new cell phone for the mess I'm in. Ally kept telling me that I needed to get this cell phone, with the fancy touch screen and internet service, until I finally caved and bought one.

I'm so busy staring at my phone that I almost don't notice when my daughter Lauren walks in. Lauren is seventeen now, smart as a whip and crazy pretty. I can't help staring at her, even as she sits in front of me this morning.

"Hey, honey. Why are you up this early?"

"Mom, don't you think we should talk about what is going on here?"

Shit, my quiet morning just ended. "I'm in quite a mess, aren't I?"

"Seriously, Mom, you need to just tell the truth."

Lauren is smarter than I am, I know that much, but she doesn't get being "in love." She doesn't understand the idea of standing by your man. I'm not sure which way to go with this conversation.

Before I decide, she blurts out, "Do you know how embarrassing this is for Jack and me? My mother, dating a kid-killer! It's bad, what they're saying about you. I need to worry about my SATs and where I'm going to college, not this bullshit!"

*Ouch.* She has a point. "I'm sorry!" I say. "This will all be over soon."

Lauren interrupts my train of thought, saying loudly, "But they say you heard what happened! What's wrong with you, Mom? Tell them what you heard!"

Every time she says "Mom" like that, I cringe. I know that she's right, but I can't tell her that I'll come clean. She isn't sure that I heard anything. Only Kat knows what I heard, and John only thinks he knows.

I lie. "I'm not sure what I heard. I need some time to wrap my head around it."

In disgust, she puts her head down onto her crossed arms lying on the table.

"It's Sunday. Go back up to bed, honey. We can talk about this later." I kiss her head. She grunts while she climbs the stairs back to her bedroom.

I squeeze my hands together into fists. *Yes! I just bought myself some more time with that one.*

I sit back down at the table to plan what I will say to my parents. Every Sunday, my mom and I call each other to chit-chat, while my dad reads the paper next to her. My mom loves hearing about all the details of the week, with my work and the kids' stuff. I'm worried that she'll be disappointed in me. She'll judge me at first, but then, hopefully, she'll remember that I'm her little girl. Won't she be on my side? I never talk to my dad on these Sunday morning calls, but I know that she relays all that I say to him, and today she will for sure.

My cell rings. I look to see who it is. It says "Mom." She beat me to it.

"Hey, Momma. What's up?"

"Hey, my Jen-girl. What are you doing?"

*My Jen-girl.* I love when she says my name that way. I take a deep breath too loudly.

Sounding alarmed, she asks, "What?"

Not "what now," but "what." My mother has always been good about not judging too quickly.

I start by saying, "I know how you feel about me dating Dylan. That he's too young and that I'm wasting my time with him."

"Yeah," she says, encouraging me to keep talking.

"Well, something bad happened."

She screeches, "Not Lauren or Jack?"

"No, no, no, they're fine. Sleeping upstairs as we speak."

"Okay, okay, go on."

I notice the change in tone. No more "my Jen-girl."

I go on to tell her the story about Dylan, and Pete's son

Tommy, and how the police think that Dylan smothered Tommy. I leave out the pocket-dial to me. I can't do it. I can't tell this woman, who thinks I'm a great mom, that I'm involved in this kid's death somehow.

My mom sighs at the end of my story, and says, "Jennifer, I never thought he was a very good guy. The way he lived on your couch and never offered you a dime!"

I'm defensive now. "I never asked him for a dime, and how does him not giving me money make him a murderer?"

"I didn't say he was a murderer, Jennifer, but if that's what you think…"

Classic. I fell right into that trap.

Frustrated more with myself than my mother, I snap, saying that one of the kids is calling for me, and that I will talk to her more about it later. I can't help myself. My mom is somewhat perfect, almost to a fault. Classy, pretty, smart, and still married to the same man after forty years. Doesn't drink or swear. She's a very private person when it comes to her family. Not like me, always telling everyone my life story. Even though my mom's life sounds peachy, it's not. My dad has been having an affair with a woman named Maureen for the last twenty-five years. It seems close to impossible to go on that long. I remember that I was around seventeen when things blew up between my parents. Things seemed bad for a long time, but then it just seemed to smooth out. We all knew he was still seeing her, but accepted it. Now I think that it was because he made such a great amount of money. After many years, I kind of got used to knowing. I've never met her. I knew he would see her at lunch during the work days, because during the summer vacations from college, I worked in his office. He would go to lunch at the same time every day. My dad and I weren't exactly pals. I was happy all the time. I laughed about everything. He's way more serious. I could really annoy him.

Mom will be really upset with me when she finds out that I have information that would put this so-called freeloading-kid-killer in jail. My dad will just roll his eyes and keep reading the paper. Before I click "end" on my cell phone my mom says, "Wait, wait a minute!" She pauses and quietly asks, "Is Dylan in jail? Are the police holding him, or is he out on bail?"

I can hear the concern in her voice. I tell her yes, and that his bail hearing is set for Monday morning.

I hear her sigh with what sounds like relief, "Okay, call me later."

Now I hit "end." I feel way worse than before. I know she will Google it and probably know more than I do in about five minutes. My mom loves all those television shows about murder mysteries. Now her daughter is one of the main characters.

# CHAPTER 7

It's Monday, and I'm happy that everyone left me alone for the rest of the day on Sunday. Kat is busy working at her greenhouse business. That's lucky for me. I know she can't wait to get back here to tell me what an idiot I am. I also know that she's right. She usually is.

The kids are still sleeping. I decide to go for a run. Not far, just my usual route of about two miles. I lace up and grab a doggie bag, because I never go running without Riley. She's always been a great running partner. She stays right beside me the whole time. I dash out the front door, remembering to lock it behind me.

My heart isn't beating smoothly. I can't get my breaths right. I start to think about Tommy. He was a skinny kid, with big brown eyes. I'd seen him a few times at the grocery store with Pete, or at the town fairs. I squish my shoulders up when I let myself think about what I heard on the phone a few days earlier. I heard Tommy die. I want to run away from all of this. I heard how ugly Dylan was to little Tommy. He was really mean, like a bully that you might see in some after-school special. It's still hard for me to believe it's true. That it really happened. I need to tell the police and Tommy's parents what I heard. I avoid Pete's house and run the other way. My heart is beating so fast, I can hear it in my head. I look behind me to see if anyone is following me. I laugh at myself a little, thinking that I watch too many murder mysteries.

I get to a cross street and am about to cross, when up comes a police car. It drives right up on the curb. The policeman puts down his window. I stop jogging and pull off my headset.

It's Pete's friend Roy. My heart jumps into my mouth, and I silently say "Fuck" under my breath. What is he is going to do to me? He steps out of the car and walks toward me. My feet feel like they're stuck in cement. He is tall and he is big.

He leans over and points at me. "You do the right thing, girl. You tell them what you heard. Get over yourself, you little bitch!"

I step back and nod my head forward. He gets back into the car and drives off.

Catching my breath is going to be impossible now. I turn around and start to walk back home. I can't wait to get home and lock this town out behind me.

When I get home, I close the front door tight behind me and lock it. Home has never felt this good. I notice that the house is still quiet, which means my kids are still sleeping. I take this time to sign onto the internet to see what I can find on Dylan, and me, for that matter. There are a few articles. Not too bad. I start to read one article from Friday on NJ.com.

**Tree Lawn Man Arrested for Smothering Policeman's Son to Death**

Tree Lawn—A Tree Lawn man has been charged with the murder of a five-year-old boy in his friend's home. Dylan Jagger, 32, was arrested Thursday morning and charged with murdering Police Officer Peter Butler's son, Thomas Butler. Deputy First Assistant Ocean County Prosecutor Michael Pappas said that Jagger is being held until his bail hearing on Monday, August 28th. Just after 5 p.m. on Wednesday night, Tree Lawn police received a 911 call that a five-year-old boy was unconscious at the home of Police Officer Peter Butler. When police and ambulances arrived, the boy was pronounced dead at the scene. Jagger is scheduled to make his initial appearance before Superior Court Judge Jacob Morsel Jr. in Tree Lawn Township on Monday.

There were a few comments from Pete's neighbors, but I'm sure that they didn't even know Dylan. I move away from the screen to get a bottle of water. At the fridge, I pause. For a second, I'd forgotten what I was in there for. I grab a water bottle and start to pace around the house. I haven't heard from Dylan. I wondered how he is doing in jail. I wonder if he has a cellmate. He obviously didn't use his one call to call me. I wonder if the police are telling him lies about me. That I'm telling them everything, and that he should just come clean. After pacing around for an hour, I can't take it any longer, so I go get my cell to call John.

"Hey, John, it's me," I whisper.

"Uh, did you decide to tell the police what you heard?" he says in his "mean voice."

"Not yet, just wondering what will happen today. Do they know he has no parents and no money? If bail is set high, he can't get out, right?" I'm suggesting that I will not be bailing him out either.

"Jen, this guy killed a kid, no joke. He needs to stay in jail." I hear voices in the background. I can tell he's covering his mouthpiece from the muffled sound.

"Okay, I know how you feel. It's clear, but is there any way I can see Dylan this week?"

"What?" he shouts.

"Really, John, I just need to see him to get closure, that's all," I lie. I want to see if Dylan still cares for me. I know that I do for him. I can't turn off my feelings just because he did something really bad. It doesn't work that way. Maybe if I go see him, I'll realize that I don't care for him anymore because of what he has done. Then I can go to the police to tell them everything I heard without feeling bad.

There is silence on the line, and I think he has hung up on me. It wouldn't be the first time.

"Jen, I will see what I can do, but know that your conversation will be recorded," he says, sounding exasperated.

Yes, I knew he could help me. He always does. I'm amused that he has warned me that the police will be recording our conversation. I watch enough Nancy Grace to know that much.

Housework has always been an escape for me. When I'm sad, or excited, or nervous, I clean. It seems like I've been cleaning for hours when John finally calls me back. It takes me a few rings to pick it up.

"Jennifer?" John questions.

"Duh, it's my number!"

I can tell he's smiling a little on the other end of the call because the pitch of his voice goes up. "Ok, I found out that Dylan is in court now. Today will not be a good time for you to see him." He can hear me sigh. "Jen, the legal process is long and drawn out. If

Dylan can't make bail, he could be in jail for a year before his court date."

A panicked feeling comes over me, like the kind I felt when I lost Lauren in a clothing store for a few minutes when she was four.

"Well, I can't wait a year to see him!" I shriek.

Frustrated by my stupidity, John mutters, "I didn't say that you couldn't see him for a year, just not today. Why do you want to see him anyway, Jen? This guy killed a little kid!"

I can't help defending Dylan. "You don't know that, they don't know that!"

John's voice goes from authoritative to almost pleading as he says, "I don't know everything they have on him, but I'm pretty sure that they are convinced he killed Tommy. Jen, please consider what you're doing to our kids."

Ignoring what John has just said, I ask, "When can I see him?"

I hear him typing on his computer, and then he reads to me, "Inmates must list information about each visitor in advance. You must be on a list of approved visitors."

I interrupt his reading. "Can he call me, or does he just get that one phone call?"

He laughs at me and explains, "Jen, it isn't the 1800s. Dylan can make phone calls from jail."

This knowledge leaves me questioning my relationship with Dylan. Why hasn't he called me? Maybe he doesn't care me for as much as I thought. Maybe the police are lying to him, and now he hates me. What am I supposed to do? How can I contact him? I feel foolish asking John to call Dylan's lawyer to tell Dylan to call me. How desperate would that look?

I sense John growing uncomfortable with the silence. "Okay, Jen. I will find out what I can. I'm just helping you in the hopes that when you see him, you won't like him anymore. You will remember what he did to Tommy, and then maybe you'll lose this infatuation."

What happened to 'innocent until proven guilty?' If he did it, I know he didn't mean to.

I try to go on another morning run. I feel like everyone is purposely not waving hello to me. Even my friend Hope, in her white Lexus, passes me and looks, but doesn't wave. The only friendly person I pass is the guy in the brown UPS truck. He smiles and waves hello. Even the guys at the car repair store don't do their usual catcalls.

I never miss my morning runs unless I'm injured. The run starts the same way every morning. For the first half-mile, my legs are stiff and heavy, but after a mile I start to feel powerful. My head clears and I feel light on my feet. Today is different. My heart pounds harder than usual and my legs are still feeling heavily weighted. It's fear that I'm feeling. I'm scared of the police. I'm afraid that someone else is going to stop me, or even run me over. What if Pete is out looking for me? What if he finds me? My stomach starts to ache. I'm sure I've got a new ulcer.

The doctors have told me I get stomach ulcers from stress. There are some things you inherit from your parents, and there are some things you learn. I inherited a bad stomach from my father, but I learned how important it is to exercise every day from him too. He is such a disciplined person. Other than his affair with Maureen, he is the most moral and fair person I know. The thought of disappointing him makes me feel terrible. I can't remember ever disappointing either of my parents, except when I divorced John. My parents love John, and to this day think I was off my rocker to leave him.

# CHAPTER 8

It's Tuesday, and I'm getting frustrated with not knowing what's going on with Dylan. I don't want to call John again, and I definitely can't call the police station. I know Kat's working at her greenhouse, but it's early enough that there won't be customers in the store yet.

I call Kat and say, "Hey, it's asshole!"

She asks, "Hey, asshole. kill anyone today?"

I can't help but laugh. "Ha-ha. Funny, Kat, as always. But really, I'm fucked up about this." I tell her what happened with the cop.

"Shit, Jen, this is getting to be too big of a fuck-up!"

I inwardly sulk and say, "I know, but—"

She quickly mimics me, "'But I love him!'"

Defensively, I respond, "I know, I know. I'm old enough to be his mother."

There's silence, the kind of pause a comedian makes to allow her to hear her applause.

"Kat, I care about him. He didn't mean to hurt this kid. Why hasn't he called me? Why am I such an idiot? I hear that if I don't tell them something soon, they're going to throw my ass in jail," I say without taking a breath.

"What? Did John tell you that?"

"No, the cop asking me all the questions at the police station kind of threatened me with that before I left. I also saw it on television somewhere. They call it 'obstruction of justice,' something about interfering with the work of police. Googled it yesterday and it says that they could stick me in jail until I talked."

Kat exclaims, "Hey, now! *That's* where you can get some action! You could be someone's bitch. *Now* we're talking!"

Annoyed with her sarcasm, I yell into the phone, "Kat!"

She recoils and says, "Okay. Okay, you need a plan. Don't say anything to the cops anymore. What did you say to make them think you know anything? Don't talk to them again unless you have to. Get to Dylan somehow and find out his side of the story. You don't even know what he says happened."

I interrupt her, "Yes, I do know what he's telling the cops. John told me that he's saying he wasn't there. That he had just walked in a minute before Tommy's father did. He's lying rather than just saying it was an accident, which I hope it was. Dylan can't be this mean. I've had him around my kids for months. I can't be that bad of a judge of character. He was always nice to my kids."

Kat jumps in, "He was a cripple, stuck on your couch! Of course, he was nice to your kids!"

"Good point."

After about twenty more minutes of conversation about her

lame boyfriend, who has been living with her off and on for eight years, we hang up. I've promised her to call when I hear anything new.

I've got to know if Dylan made bail. Is he roaming the streets? I peer out the window. I want to know if he thinks that I betrayed him. I also want to know how the police knew about his call to my cell phone. I assume that they took his phone from him, but how did they know whether we were actually talking to each other? I think he must have said that he wasn't talking to anyone before he got to Pete's house. He would be telling the truth if he didn't know that he pocket-dialed me.

I decide to eat crow and ask John about Dylan again, by text this time. He scares me a little when he's mad. I text him and ask if Dylan made bail. A second goes by before he texts back, *Yes!*

I text him back, *How?* He writes back, *His step-father put up his house.* I rush to ask, *Then where is he?* Oh god, I realize how ridiculous that must sound to my ex-husband, but before I can beat myself up too much, he smugly texts back, *You won't be hearing from him because I was at the hearing and told him to stay the fuck away from you, the house, and my kids.*

I feel like I just got slapped.

This was supposed to be a fun tryst for me. A cute man to have fun, un-emotional sex with. How has this happened? John thinks I brought a child-killer into my kids' lives. I will be known forever as the cougar who found herself a baby-killer. Ugh!

*Bing!* Oh God. Another text, but this time it's not from John. It's a number that I don't know. I immediately think it's another cop trying to ream me. I look, and it says, *You there?*

What? Am I where? I text back, *Sorry, who is this?* There is a long wait for the next text, and I find myself thinking about why women always say they are sorry. Why are we always sorry? Kat wouldn't have started with "sorry."

I've lost my train of thought. I look over to a picture on the mantel. It's of me and my little man, Kev, sitting on the sand on the beach. His mom had taken the shot of us last summer. I watch a little boy during the school year. I've been caring for him since his birth. Needless to say, I love this little fella like one of my own. *Oh, shit!* I realize that I haven't spoken to his mother about this fiasco. They go away the same week each year to Aruba with his grandparents. I'm thankful that they're still away. She'll definitely think I'm nuts not to turn Dylan in. She'll say, 'It's a kid we're talking about here, Jen!' *Ugh.* I walk into the kitchen, shaking the thought out of my head.

*Bing!* "Oh, shit!" The sound is like an electric shock to me. I look at my phone. It's the number with no name. It says, *can we talk?*

*Shit!* This must be Dylan. He must not want to say that it's him. I wonder if they have a bug on my phone, or if they're watching my texts. I nod, thinking that that would make sense. Assuming that it's Dylan, I text back, *sure.*

*Bing!* Another text pops up: *lol ok where we met that time near the school at 1 a.m. Ok? I will be there around 3.*

I think, *What school? What school at 1 a.m.?* Then I remember. I feel stupid for not knowing right away, but now I feel shame. That was the time I made a booty call to him in the middle of the night. We had met at the school's playground. We had had sex on the slide. Oh god, I'm *ridiculous.* I had sex on a slide, at a fucking elementary school, no less. Kat had a holiday with that one. I heard sex-on-a-slide jokes for weeks. *I'm* the one who needs to be in jail. I text him, *ok.*

I look at the clock. It's already 1 p.m. I only have two hours. I need to get pretty. I run up to the shower. While in the shower, I remember the time that I stepped in to help Dylan wash after he broke his knee. It started very innocently, me helping him shower. I had wrapped a garbage bag around his soft cast and duct-taped it to his thigh. I figured that was the only way for water to not get in there. Bad move on my part. It hurt him when it came to take the duct-tape off. *Oops.* The fact that this makes me laugh now concerns me. Maybe I'm losing that loving feeling.

Well anyway, back to the good thoughts. There he was, this smoking hot babe in my shower. I was leaning down, washing his good thigh. Up and down, with the soap in my hand. He was holding his head back in the shower to wet his hair. At that moment, I got all wet from the run-off from his hair. He laughed and said, "Just get naked and get in." It was weird. I was in "mom-mode." It took me but a minute to think, *Why not?* I disrobed and stepped in. I felt a little shy at first, as it was rather bright in the bathroom. But all those insecurities fell away when he wrapped his arm around my bare back and started kissing my neck. Oh Lord, how I remember how hot that was. I put my head back under the shower head and try to remember how good it felt to be stroked and kissed by him. He was so young and beautiful.

*Ouch.* The water scorches me back to reality. Someone must have flushed a toilet in the house. The kids must be up. I get out of the shower and think of what I'm going to tell the kids. I try not to get too dolled-up. No perfume. I brush on mascara and add a bit of blush onto my cheeks. I hang upstairs until 2:30, hoping to avoid my kids. I hear Jack go out the front door to football practice. One of his buddies drives, and is nice enough to pick him up for practice every day.

What will I ask Dylan? I feel funny accusing him of killing Tommy, even though I know that he did. I wish that I could forget what I heard. I wish that last Wednesday, I had ignored the call from Dylan. Maybe it was divine intervention that the cell called me. Something wanted me to know. Maybe it was a test. My head is spinning when I suddenly realize that it's 2:45 p.m. I've got to go meet Dylan. I feel excited, but also petrified.

I pull up to a parking spot in the restaurant next to the school. It's summer time, and I know that there are no kids, but maybe the secretary or someone is there. I don't want anyone to see me meeting with Dylan, the child-killer. I sit and watch the playground set. I see the slide that we had sex on. I hear Kat in my head, teasing me about the slide. *Why on earth do I tell her these things, knowing she'll abuse me?* Maybe I know that I deserve the ridicule.

I see him. He's in a sweatshirt with the hood up. It's eighty-nine degrees out, so he looks out-of-place. He looks creepy, walking towards the playground with his hands in his pockets and his head forward, like a pedophile. I don't lose sight of him as I open my car door and start to walk toward him. He turns toward me and smiles.

Man, is he cute! How could that sweet face hurt a fly? But then I remember Tommy's cries, and my hair stands up on my neck. I suddenly feel a sense of panic. I didn't tell anyone I was meeting Dylan. I knew what they would say. Now I feel like I might be in danger.

As I walk towards him, I keep pushing my hair behind my ears and biting my lower lip, exhibiting both of my nervous habits. My heart is pounding. I still like him so much! As I get closer, I open my arms. He seems relieved by this, and steps forward and embraces me. He pulls me in close to his chest and whispers, "I'm sorry."

My body stiffens up. I step back and ask, "For what?"

I can hear that I'm yelling. He makes a shushing gesture, with his finger to his lips. I hate when anyone does that to me.

His head lowers, and he quietly says, "What do you think you heard? I didn't know that I had pocket-dialed you. Why were you listening?"

Placing the blame on me flicks a switch, and I feel my temper flaring. I start accusing him, "Why the fuck did you hurt Tommy like that? What the fuck were you thinking? Why did you lie to the police? Why didn't you say you were just playing around and it was an accident?"

His head jerks back at each question. He says nothing when I stop, and just stares at me. I feel unsure of my footing. He has no expression on his face: not frowning, not smiling. He's like a mannequin. Suddenly, he turns and starts to walk away. Is he walking away from *me*? I'm the one trying to protect him.

Maybe I surprised him. Maybe he didn't know that I heard it all. He just keeps walking as I stand here next to the slide, dumfounded. I can't move. I feel like I've played my hand, and lost. It feels like I've overdone it, again. I go back to my car and just sit and cry. I'm not sure why, but it feels expected. I should turn right and go straight to the police to tell them what I heard. But of course, I turn left, towards home. I need more time to think.

# CHAPTER 9

It has only been thirty minutes since I told Lauren that I was going out to meet Kat. I need to come up with a reason for why I'm back this soon. I peek around the door and see Lauren, sitting on the stairs with her head in her hands. Worried, I hurry to her side.

"What's up, honey?'

She looks up at me with swollen eyes. "Mom, you have to do something about this situation! You need to take care of it. You need to tell them what they want to hear. What did you hear?"

"Lauren, I didn't hear anything."

She scrunches her face up at me in disgust, but still looks pretty. Lauren was one of the lucky ones: born with big blue eyes, long, lean legs, and wavy blonde hair. She's also smart as hell, like her father. She's almost perfect. I'm her one flaw. Married two times, divorced two times, and now this. I need to tell her. I rarely lie to her about anything. I sit closer to her and whisper, "Okay."

"Dylan pocket-dialed me when he was at Pete's house. I heard Dylan roughhousing with Tommy. I listened to Dylan kill Tommy."

Putting my hands over my face, I whine, "How could Dylan be that mean?"

Lauren raises her hand. I stop. "Mom, there was an instance once when he snapped at Jack."

Surprised, I ask, "When, and for what? Jack has at least thirty pounds on him."

She puts her hand out like she's holding a remote. "Jack came home and was in the kitchen. I guess he hadn't seen Dylan on the chair over there. He must have been sleeping because when Jack turned on the TV, Dylan snapped. Jack said he was crazy pissed-off."

With that, I lay back on the stairs. *Ugh, what did I bring into our house, into our lives?*

Lauren leans over and puts her head on my shoulder. "It'll be okay. Just tell them what you told me."

"I can't yet." I say.

I feel a chill as she jumps to her feet and runs up the stairs. She slams her door. The house shudders a bit. That girl doesn't know how powerful she can be. Last month she surprised me by participating in a mini-triathlon. I had no idea that she had such endurance.

The day drags on. I'm so sad. All I can think about is that Dylan doesn't like me anymore. I know that's wrong, making it all about me. I should be thinking about what happened. How I heard him teasing and taunting Tommy. How I heard a muffled cry, like Dylan was sitting on Tommy. Now Dylan knows what I heard.

John had told me that I was the only witness. He said that our phones were linked for the seven minutes before Pete got home from work. I'm so fucking stupid. I should have said that I wasn't listening. I can't even remember what I said to the officers when they came to the front door. My big mouth has always annoyed my mother. She would always tell me when someone at the country club knew *all* of my business because I had told her at the nail salon. She would say, "Jennifer, keep your life story to yourself." She was right, of course. I probably wouldn't be in this predicament right now if I had kept my trap shut. *Dammit!*

My cell rings. It's Kat, thank God.

"Hey, girl. What's up?"

"What's up with stupid-ass?" she asks.

"I saw him today."

"Who? The kid-killer?"

I sigh. "Yes."

"Did he confess?"

"Nope, nothing. But as usual, I said too much."

Kat screeches, "Why did you say anything to him? You don't owe him anything. I don't understand you at all! He was a cute piece, that's all. It's not like you love him. Think of the damage you're doing to your kids. If your parents find out that you can put this guy away and aren't, they'll think you're an ass!"

I mull this over in my head. "Okay, okay! I need to sit and write down what I remember. If I just hand it to the police, maybe I don't have to talk to them. I'm just worried that if I go there, I'll make things worse for myself somehow."

Kat interrupts, "What if Mr. Child-Killer knows that you're

the only witness that can put him away? Don't you think you should worry about what he might do? Like fucking *kill* you?"

"Kat, he wouldn't hurt me," I intercede.

She jumps back in. "You ass! He killed a kid. Not by accident, like you're trying to convince yourself, but on purpose. He must have known that the kid couldn't breathe. You said you thought he might have been sitting on him. He didn't say those hideous things by accident!"

She's screaming at me. I can't blame her, but I'm getting angry. She usually calls me an ass as a joke, but now it seems like she means it.

"I'll ask John what to do." I say shortly, hoping it will end this conversation.

Backing off, she says, "Fine. Call me after you speak with him."

*Click.*

# CHAPTER 10

Before I get the chance to decide what to do next, my cell rings. It's John.

"Hey, what's up?"

John mutters, "Hey, I've been talking to the captain." I assume he means the police captain, Tony Bellizoni.

He continues, "He thinks that even if you heard Dylan kill Tommy, it won't be enough to convict him. He wants you to wear a wire and get him to confess." He says the last part quickly, as if knowing I would freak out next.

"That's nuts! That'd be so embarrassing, having all the boys at the station listening in on my private life. Getting good laughs over everything I say and do. No fucking way!"

John breaths heavily into the phone in frustration. "Jen, this guy is going to get away with killing a little boy. You love kids! That's why you left finance to watch kids for a living. You can't possibly like Dylan enough to protect him."

After seeing Dylan today, he might be right. "Okay, what if I write down everything I heard and let that be that?"

Exasperated, John says, "You do that tonight, and we can bring over your statement tomorrow. I have court in the morning. Let's plan on early afternoon."

I smirk. There he goes again, never committing to a time. One of the cracks in our marriage. John used to always say he would be home at a certain time, then walk in the door hours later. It drove me nuts. He's gotten smarter, knowing to use "before" or "after" his stated time, now.

I agree, and we hang up.

I realize it's dinner time. The award for 'mother of the year' is out of reach, but I can at least make sure they don't go hungry. I go with spaghetti with turkey burger meat sauce: my go-to meal.

While waiting for the water to boil, I run around looking for a pen and paper. I close my eyes, trying to remember exactly what I heard. This is bigger than me. I try to convince myself that if I just write it all down, my troubles will go away. *He* will go away, and so will my happiness.

I'll write down what I heard, but that doesn't mean I'll hand it over. I begin to mull over all the various outcomes. The police will conclude that it was an accident, or Dylan will go to jail for twenty years. Dimple-faced, blue-eyed Dylan.

Dinner is ready. I bang the wall at the end of the stairs to get the kids attention. "Dinner!" I call.

Lauren and Jack stampede down the stairs, seeming sullen and grumpy. I remind myself that they're teenagers.

"What's up, Mom?" Jack asks.

Leave it to boys to act like nothing's wrong. I go with it.

"Nothing."

Lauren rolls her eyes.

We belly up to our bowls of spaghetti in silence.

They hate me. Who could blame them? Their own mom, dating a way-younger guy. Letting him live on their couch, and now protecting him after he killed a kid. I can't stand the hush in the room.

I burst out, "Okay listen, kids. I plan to write down what I heard Dylan do. Dad's picking me up tomorrow to bring me over to the station. I'm going to answer their questions."

Tears roll down my cheeks. My hands are shaking. I'm overwhelmed with remorse.

"I'm sorry that it's taken me this long. I just liked being with Dylan too much. I can't believe I did this to you! I'm so sorry! I'm so sorry!"

Lauren reaches out her hand to cover mine. "Mom, I know this sucks for you, but you need to do the right thing here."

She's just like her dad when it comes to following the rules. He used to say often, "You have a responsibility to always tell the truth."

He didn't know that I was teaching them to lie. I told them the importance of eye contact and standing tall. Unconventional teaching, yes, but the world is full of shameless liars. They needed to learn how to recognize it, and better yet, how to lie. Just last year during finals, Lauren had used her lying skills to postpone her history final.

I can tell Jack feels uneasy at the table. He keeps tapping his foot. "Mom and a guy" is never what he wants to talk about. He quickly finishes dinner and asks to be excused. Up the stairs he goes, two at a time, without another word.

I look back at Lauren. My lovely Lauren. She asked me once to describe her in one word. After some thought, I said, 'lovely.' She was pleased with that answer. My dad would have chosen 'annoying' for me.

"Lauren, do you think you could help me write what Dad called a 'witness statement?'" She leaps up from her chair. "Sure, let me Google it."

This lifts my mood. Lauren Googles everything, to the point that her friends have nicknamed her "Google." They always say, "She knows everything—just ask her."

"All that reading she does. That's why she is so smart!" my mother would say.

When she was little, Lauren and I would go into the town's book store, Tree Lawn Books, and she would point and say, "Read it. Read it. Read it."

Lauren comes back armed with the information we need. She slides in next to me. "Witness statement: Name of case. Your full name and address. What you saw, or rather, what you heard. They want you to number each paragraph. After that, it says to write: 'I believe that the facts stated in the witness statement are true.' Then sign and date." She smiles. "You've got this, Mom."

"Okay, I'll write down what I remember, and try to make believe this isn't Dylan I'm talking about."

Frowning, Lauren places her hand on my forearm, "Mom,

there are plenty of fish in the sea. This one just happens to be a freaking *piranha*. I'll let you figure this out." She laughs as she cascades back up the stairs, then yells back, "Call me if you need me."

She's a gift from God.

I write down my name and address. I don't know "case name," other than Dylan's name. I write that at the top of the page. I start to pour out what I remember on paper. The cell ringing. Seeing Dylan's name pop up. No one on the line. Dylan talking to Tommy. Hearing some cries from Tommy. The ugly words Dylan said to him. More cries, this time muffled. How I didn't know what to do. Dylan saying, "How about this, Tommy? Does this hurt? Are you scared, Tommy?" I describe the tone of Dylan's voice. How he sounded creepy and mean. Then the silence that followed. No more cries. No more pleads to stop. Silence. How I thought that maybe the phone call had ended. And then, moments later, still holding the cell to my ear, hearing Pete yell, "What's wrong with Tommy? Why is he blue?"

How I heard Dylan lie, "I don't know, I just got here." I sit back and take a deep breath.

Stinking liar.

I number my paragraphs. I write that my statement is true. I sign and date, feeling at peace. Sorrow and grief take over my heart. I'll never know if Dylan ever loved me. If I turn this in, he'll hate me. *I* would hate me. I try to clear my head of exhaustion. I need sleep.

# CHAPTER 11

Wind and rain hits my bedroom window at 5 a.m., waking me up. I roll around, trying to go back to sleep, but after a few flips of my pillow, I give up. I go downstairs and see Riley wagging her tail. To be a happy dog, with not a worry in the world! I grab a cup of tea and sit down in front of my laptop: my daily ritual. The first thing I do these days is type "Dylan Jagger" into the search bar. Today, I find related stories; one contains Tommy Butler's obituary and information about his funeral. Next, I type in "Jennifer Burns." My Facebook, Instagram, and Twitter pop up, but no new news. Thankfully, I haven't been reported as a witness.

After a bowl of Cheerios, I don my running gear. The news hasn't reported me as a witness, but everyone in this town knows. I can hear it now: "two-time divorcee screwing some young guy who killed a kid." I might as well have done it myself.

Running up my street, I'm met by a neighbor pulling their garbage pail out to the curb. Damn, I forgot it was garbage day. Staring down at the street, I run by. No words are exchanged. Relieved, I pick my head up and run a bit faster, eager to get this over with.

Running used to be my escape. Now, all I can think about is Dylan. I still want him. I loved being with him. I loved his hands all over me. He was aggressive and a little rough, but I liked it. Bruises would sometimes appear the day after we had sex, like a badge of honor. Sometimes, though, he could be a little too rough. A few times it was too much for me. We had a safe word now.

When I told my therapist, Dr. Thorne, about how I liked it when Dylan got rough with me during sex, she asked me point-blank, "Have you ever been sexually assaulted?"

"Yes." I had said, "I was date-raped by someone when I was in high school."

When Dr. Thorne started to ask me for details, I couldn't answer. I felt frozen. Dr. Thorne pried no further, and asked me to find a safe, quiet place when I got home to write down my story. At the next appointment, I handed her this letter:

> I am a survivor of a sexual assault. It took me from the time of the assault thirty-two years ago to be able to say that I am a survivor. For fifteen years, I felt more like the victim. I was seventeen years old. An innocent, joyful senior girl. It was the 4th of July, 1984. I was excited to be going on a date with the varsity basketball player of a rival high school. He was so athletic and handsome, I couldn't believe he liked me. That evening, this charming, handsome boy took me to his room after the fireworks and raped me. I cried and said no, over and over again, but he didn't stop. I went silent. For five years after, I was silent about what he did to me. I never even spoke to him about what he had done to me during that time. I was scared. I was ashamed. I was embarrassed. I felt pitiful. He took my innocence from me. He took from me my savor for life. I told no one for five years. He

knew he had wronged me. He knew he had hurt me. I was convinced of that. I quietly cried every day. It was an attack on not only my body, but my soul, for fifteen years. Then, one day, I saw him in a bar. I felt strong enough to approach him. I was an adult. I pulled up the courage to ask him if we could sit down and talk about what happened to me that fateful night. He said yes. I was happy. I know that seems crazy, but I was and am still appreciative that he, my assailant, was willing to talk to me about what he did to me. I met him at his house a week later with a six pack of beer in tow. I sat across the room from him. He sat slumped over, head down, as I asked him questions about that horrible life altering night. He answered every question honestly. He said he heard my cries for him to stop. He said that when I went silent, he thought I started enjoying myself. He said he was wrong. He said he was very sorry. I walked into that night a victim and walked out a survivor. I am thankful, to this day, for his honest, candid answers to my storm of questions about the night he raped me. I am now at peace with what he did to me, but it took many years. I was one of the lucky ones that got to hear the words, "I'm sorry."

Dr. Thorne silently read it in front of me. When she was done, she put the paper down, stood, and hugged me. She said it was brave to have told her my story. She said that I was not alone, that many girls have had similar experiences, and that I was lucky to have been able to question my assailant. She seemed very impressed, and that made me feel less embarrassed.

Many meetings with Dr. Thorne helped me come to the realization that a lot of my sadness still came from that horrible incident. I remember thinking that time doesn't always heal old wounds.

Thinking about this now brings tears to my eyes. Maybe that's why I was so quick to forgive Dylan. After all, I forgave the man who raped me.

These memories make my breathing too quick. I decide to run the shorter route back home.

# CHAPTER 12

It's a little after 1 p.m. when John knocks at the door. Since he lived here for nine years, I'm sure it's still weird for him to knock, even though we've been divorced for thirteen years. How time flies by. I hope today flies by, too.

I open the door to see what Kat would call his "resting bitch face." Kat loves to make fun of people's RBF. John's is a big frown. I giggle, thinking of Kat's impersonation of him.

"Hey, John."

John immediately gets to the point. "You ready? Do you have your witness statement?"

"Yes, *Dad*."

John grimaces and turns towards his car. I follow.

While putting on my seatbelt, I ask, "Does this make you my lawyer?"

He puts out his hand. "If you pay me."

I throw a dollar into his hand. "Hired!"

As we walk into the Tree Lawn Police station, I feel all eyes on me. When I was younger, I dreamed of being famous, but not now. I even hate being recognized by my kids' friends' parents. I never know what to say. Kat calls me an extraverted-introvert.

I find myself grabbing John's elbow. Scared and feeling under siege, I start to panic. John grabs onto my hand and whispers, "You'll be all right."

John has always known when he needs to be extra nice to me. I think he thinks I'm fragile. Normally I wouldn't agree with him, but right now he's right.

The officer asks me and John to follow him down the hall to a room with a table topped with a mic and four chairs. I quickly sit in the closest one. John pulls a chair from the table and sits back near the wall, and the officer sits in front of me. He begins to transcribe everything we say.

**Police:** State your name and address.

**Jennifer Burns:** Jennifer Burns, 15 Duncan Lane, Tree Lawn, NJ

**Police:** Do you know why you're here today?

**Jennifer Burns:** About what I heard last Tuesday.

**Police:** I understand you're a witness to this murder?

**Jennifer:** Yes, I was listening on my phone.

**Police:** Were you the only person listening on the phone that day?

**Jennifer Burns:** Yes.

**Police:** Are you okay to answer some questions for me?

**Jennifer Burns:** Sure. I don't know how much help I'll be. A lot of what I heard was muffled.

**Police:** Do you know the suspect, Dylan Jagger?

**Jennifer Burns:** Yes, we've been dating for five months.

**Police:** Do you know the victim, Tommy Butler?

**Jennifer Burns:** Yes, I said hello a few times at county fairs or in town.

**Police:** Would you say you can recognize Dylan's voice?

**Jennifer Burns:** Yes.

**Police:** Would you say that you can recognize Tommy's voice?

**Jennifer Burns:** No. But Dylan kept saying his name.

**Police:** Did you hear any other voices?

**Jennifer Burns:** Yes, Pete Butler's.

**Police:** What did you hear him say?

**Jennifer Burns:** He asked what was wrong with Tommy. He asked where Christine was, and said that she should be watching him. Someone yelled to call 911. I don't know who.

**Police**: What else did you hear between Dylan and Tommy?

**Jennifer Burns**: Dylan asked Tommy if what he was doing to him hurt, and if he was scared. It sounded like he was smothering him.

**Police**: What makes you say that?

**Jennifer Burns:** Their voices were clear at first, but as the call went on, Tommy's voice sounded muffled. Like it was being covered up. I could hear Tommy crying, and telling him to stop.

**Police**: Can you describe the tone of Dylan's voice?

**Jennifer Burns:** Direct, mean, angry, and scary.

**Police:** Was the voice you heard loud?

**Jennifer Burns:** No, I wouldn't say he was loud.

**Police:** Do you think Dylan knew you were listening?

**Jennifer Burns:** I know he didn't know, because when I met up with him yesterday, he acted surprised.

**Police**: You met him yesterday? Why?

**Jennifer Burns:** I wanted to know why he hurt Tommy.

**Police:** You mean killed Tommy?

**Jennifer Burns:** Yes. But he didn't say anything except that he was sorry.

**Police:** Sorry for what?

Jennifer Burns: Just sorry.

**Police:** We would like to bug your cell phone.

**Jennifer Burns:** Okay.

I sign the interview statement.

The police officer says, "John tells me that you have a witness statement."

I pull it from my pocket and hand it over. "Yes, here it is."

He unfolds it and reads for a moment, then looks up at me. "Are you willing to help us, Ms. Burns?"

I dig my hands into my front pockets. "Maybe?"

The officer explains that Dylan won't know that I was here today. He won't find out that I told them anything. He wants Dylan to think that I forgive him, that I'm on his side. He says that they are one hundred percent sure that Dylan killed Tommy, but now they need to find out why. What was his motive? He starts talking about bugging my phone and house.

I interrupt, "Not my house."

He looks over at John with his eyes wide open, then tilts his head and looks back at me. "Fine." He puts out his hand, palm up. Assuming he wants my cell phone, I retrieve it from my back pocket and place it down in his hand.

"I'll be right back." He says, pointing down the hall. "Wait in the front hall."

John and I sit down in the chairs in the front of the police station. Feeling like a criminal myself, I look over at John and ask, "How did I do?"

Smiling, he answers, "Jen, you did great. You did the right thing. But—and you're not going to like this—I want the kids to stay with me until this is all over."

I jump to my feet. "No way, John! I need those kids. I won't let him in the house. I'm just going to talk to him."

He breathes in deeply. "For now, they will stay with me. Okay?"

I feel powerless. "Okay. For now."

The officer brings me back my phone and says, "We're all set."

I take the phone and look at it. It looks the same.

He pulls out his card and hands it to me. "Please call us with any updates."

# CHAPTER 13

I need a Kat fix. I text her that we need some "porch time" tonight. During the planning phase of our house, John and I had decided on a wraparound porch. It's Kat's favorite place. We can hang in the overstuffed chairs drinking beer for hours. One day we sat for eleven straight hours, waiting for a big storm that never came.

Kat texts back, *Oh, I will be there!*

I need to tell Kat all that has transpired. I always tell her everything. She's a vault. No matter what I tell Kat, she makes a joke about it, but she'll never repeat it to anyone.

Kat shows up earlier than I expect. I greet her at the door, with her dog at her knee.

She smells her shirt. "Sorry that I stink. I came right from the greenhouse." She goes over to one of the big chairs and sits down. "I can't wait to hear what's going on. You still protecting Jeffrey Dahmer?"

I frown at her. "You're hysterical."

Kat puts a hand up. "Okay, okay. What happened since we last spoke?"

I grab a few beers from the fridge and come back out. After handing her a beer, I sit down. I start to tell her about the witness statement that Lauren helped me with, when Kat interrupts and says,

"If Lauren helped you, we know it was done right. Next?"

I sigh. "John drove me to have my interview with the police."

Kat laughs. "I wish I had an ex-husband to take care of me."

I continue, "It was just like what you see on any crime show. One room with a darkened window, four chairs, and a table with a mic on it. John sat behind me, and the cop asked me a bunch of questions."

Kat smirks. "Was it that hot cop married to Ashley's sister?"

I snap. "No! Shut up and let me finish! Obviously, the police were recording the interview, because within minutes, the cop had a statement of the interview for me to sign. And yes, I gave him my written witness statement."

"So, are you all done with this shit now?" Kat asks.

I hold up my cell. "Nope. They bugged my cell."

Kat jumps up and grabs my cell. "What the fuck? The cops bugged it? Why haven't you warned me? What if I'd called you saying that I just killed Scott and to bring a shovel?"

I frown. "Why is everything always about you?"

Kat flips the cell over, back and forth. "I see nothing. Where's the bug?"

"Who knows? They also wanted to bug this house, but I said no.'

Still searching my cell, Kat asks, "They think you can get him to confess on the phone? Really? No one, not even Dylan, is that stupid."

"The cop says that they need a motive, I guess so that they can prosecute him. They want me to keep seeing him, and they're keeping the fact that I gave them a statement quiet."

Kat laughs out loud. "So, you're telling me that the police asked you to keep screwing this guy so you can get dirt on him?"

I shrug. "Not in so many words, but yes."

Kat throws both hands up and pleads, "Jesus, Jen, are you nuts?"

I can't help being defensive. "Kat, he never hurt me. He doesn't know about me going to the police, and it's not like I'll hate it."

Kat shakes her head and talks to her dog. "Brandy, did you hear that? Cougar here is going to keep having sex with Mr. Killjoy."

Kat answers in her dog's voice. "Like fucks for facts?"

Kat laughs at her own joke, looking down at Brandy. "Exactly!"

"Oh God, stop! Really! Listen!" I wave to get Kat's attention. "There are a few things that don't make sense here. Wouldn't the police think we were talking to each other during that phone call? The line was open for at least five minutes. That sounds more like a conversation than a pocket dial."

Hand to chin. Kat says, "You have a point. Has Pete reached out to you? Was he there during the police interview?"

"No," I answer. "And he wasn't even at the station. I haven't heard a word from him. Don't you think that's odd?"

Kat leans towards me. "Yes! I'd be all up in your face."

Sarcastically, I ask, "Yeah, like you're such a bad ass?"

After a few beers I ask Kat, "Do you think you could kill

someone?"

She thinks for a moment. "Yes, if someone came after me, my family, a friend, or especially Brandy." She pets Brandy's head. "I think it's something that you decide in the moment. But I wouldn't kill someone out of spite. He'd have to be coming at me, or them. What about you?"

I pucker my lips and rub my chin. "If someone was harassing Lauren or Jack, making them feel unsafe, I might have a little talk with them. Remember that kid that was harassing Lauren freshman year? I told her friends to tell him that if he kept it up, I would be outside his house with a bat." We start to laugh, but I almost immediately stop, remembering how serious this situation really is. "I can't get Tommy's cries out of my head. If Dylan had hurt Lauren or Jack, yes, I would kill him."

We crack open a few more beers and devise a plan. Kat says I should wait for Dylan to contact me first. I'll be nice and consoling. If he tells me how sorry he is, I'll pretend to understand. When he claims that it was an accident, I'll agree. I need him to trust me. I tell Kat that I can do this, but the truth is, I *want* to do this. Not for the truth, not for Tommy, but for myself. I miss him. Common sense tells me to hate him, but my heart can't let him go. Not talking to him makes my chest hurt. Hearing his name over and over again gives me goose bumps. I miss the warmth of his body next to me. I want to smell his neck, and taste his soft lips. The idea of having sex with him again doesn't scare me, but I wonder if it will be the same. When he gets a little rough now, will I be frightened? Will I be able to be in the moment, and not think about what I heard him say?

# CHAPTER 14

It's a new day. I didn't get much sleep last night. I never do when I drink too much, but the fun I've had with Kat outweighs the night of insomnia. I can't do it often, or I would never sleep. Hoping to see a text from Dylan, I check my phone. Yes, there is a text from that odd number again. I press on the text, and see enough to know that he wants to see me.

*"Hey Jen. I miss you. Can we get together? I know things are not good right now. Please tell me when I can come over to talk.*

Immediately, I write back, *"Come by tonight around 8p.m. I miss you too."*

Realizing that the police can see my texts makes me feel embarrassed and ashamed. My hope is that they'll think that I'm only seeing him to get more information out of him.

*Bing!* I look again. *I will be there. Can't wait to hold you.*

I squeal with delight and text him back, *See you then.*

When I get nervous, I clean. By the end of the day, this house will be immaculate. I walk the dog. Water the plants. Go for a run. I pull out the vacuum, and then the wet Swiffer. I Windex the windows. Since the kids are at their dad's house, I can be loud. I crank the volume up on the radio. My mind rotates through images of Dylan smiling at me, to what Tommy must have looked like in his coffin, to Dylan being handcuffed in court, being escorted into prison. *This can't be real,* I think. It's like I crave his sweetness. He's like a drug to me. I try to convince myself that if I figure out that Dylan meant to kill Tommy, we'll be over.

Suddenly desperate to see Dr. Thorne, I call to see if she can see me today. Yes, she's had a cancellation. Dr. Thorne's surname doesn't fit her. She's far from prickly. There's a softness to her, and she doesn't appear to judge me. The air around her is calm and peaceful, something I'm not.

I'm thankful that I found her. I remember how I searched for a good therapist after my first divorce. Someone who would understand me. I decided I needed a female therapist after I met with two different male therapists who both left me feeling violated. They didn't do or say anything specific; it was just an uncomfortable feeling I would get while telling them stories about my relationships with men. It felt like they enjoyed them more than they should.

I'm early to my appointment. The soothing music she plays in her waiting room is nice and calming. A door opens, and a girl with bloodshot eyes walks out. She has been crying.

Dr. Thorne comes through the door and extends her hand.

"Boy, do I need to see you," I say, shaking it.

Smiling, she says, "Come on in. Tell me what's going on."

Memories flash through my mind, of other times I've been in this room. Dr. Thorne has helped me so much. I'd waited thirty years to seek help after my sexual assault. She said that my anxiety and some of my depression was because of never getting treatment. She wished that I'd gotten help earlier in my life, because then I would know that most of the things I was doing and feeling were symptoms of Post-Traumatic Stress Disorder. No one was there to tell me that crying after sex was normal for someone who experienced what I had. Sex was a bit confusing to me for a long time. Did I like it? Did I hate it? Dr. Thorne had helped spell out all of those confusing feelings.

I make eye contact. "Dr. Thorne, have you heard about the little boy who died in Tree Lawn last week?"

"Yes, that was horrible," she answers. "Poor boy."

Looking away, I say, "You know the younger man that I've been seeing? Well… he's involved in his death."

She puts her hand up to her mouth. "Oh, Jen, that must be horrible for you! I know how much you like him."

I tilt my head. "It gets worse."

Dr. Thorne's eyes widen as she leans in.

Trembling, I whisper, "I heard him kill him."

She asks, "What do you mean you heard it?"

"He pocket-dialed me by accident while it was happening. I heard everything. Dr. Thorne, I didn't know what to do. I should have hung up and called the police, but I didn't know it would end this badly. Anyway, they know what I heard now. I gave a witness statement."

I told the truth, but now I feel horrible. I feel horrible for the boy and his family. I feel horrible for my kids. I feel horrible for

Dylan, and I feel confused and ashamed that I still care for him. I miss him. I know I shouldn't. The police want me to keep seeing him. They say they need a motive. But the truth is, I *want* to see him. Dr. Thorne, what's wrong with me?"

Dr. Thorne looks up from the scribble on her pad and says, "What you're experiencing is called 'unconditional love.' It's like a mother's love; 'I love you no matter what happens.' Most parents feel it for their children. Would you still love Lauren or Jack if they had committed this crime?"

"Yes!"

"Don't feel shame or guilt about still caring for him. After Dylan injured his leg, you became his caregiver. You formed a maternal love for him. Also, you're fifteen years his senior," she explains.

The crease in her forehead deepens as she says, "What I'm more concerned for is your safety, if you continue to date him. If you're not sure if he meant to kill him or not, you could be in danger. Being evil isn't easy. The human brain is coded for compassion. If he hasn't shown this kind of lack of care for human life before, then it's more than likely that he didn't mean to kill that little boy. But the question here is whether he's behaved this way before. You've told me that he likes to have rough sex. He likes to dominate you. Some men receive pleasure from the physical or psychological pain of their girlfriend. Does this make him a murderer? I don't know, but you need to be careful."

We work together on ways to cope with what is going on. How to talk to Jack and Lauren about it, to ask them questions on how this is affecting them. To listen, and to tell them that their feelings matter. We agree to tell them about the police bugging my cell phone, but to involve them as little as possible. And to only see Dylan when they are at their father's house. All this talk of my kids makes me cry. It makes me realize that what I do can have a lasting effect on many other people. It's not like when I was single, and could be out all night, see who I wanted, bring home who I wanted. I wish I could act my age. But I was just so bored before Dylan came around.

We make a date for our next session and say our goodbyes. Right before the door closes behind me, Dr. Thorne says, "Be careful, and call me if you need me."

## CHAPTER 15

For the rest of the day, I find myself needing to take a lot of deep breaths. My anxiety level is higher than normal. I'm not sure if it's because I'm excited to see Dylan, or because I'm dreading the idea. Will I still be attracted to him? Will sex be different? Will he try to hurt me? Will he confess to me? He's no longer perched up on that pedestal I put him on.

Both kids are at their father's house. John and I have agreed for them to stay there until this situation is settled. It's inconvenient for Lauren, due to the high number and weight of her school books. She complains that we're being overly cautious. Jack, on the other hand, goes without a word. I don't think he cares where he sleeps as long as he has his Xbox.

All this uncertainty is making me depressed. Nothing feels the same any more. Even running to the grocery store felt different. I worry about who I might see, about whether people I know might ask too many questions, or if strangers will sneer at me.

Inside, the grocery store is bustling. No one pays me any mind. I start to relax, and grab bananas, apples, grapes, and oranges. The colors of the fruits brighten up the kitchen. As I push the grocery cart into the next aisle, I almost collide with someone.

"Sorry!" I say automatically.

A girl with brown hair trailing down her back turns. "No problem," She says, then turns back to look at the cereal boxes.

To my surprise, it's Christine, the girl who was supposed to be babysitting Tommy the day he died. She doesn't appear to recognize me.

"Are you Christine?" I ask.

She looks back at me, tensing. "Yes…why?" She asks suspiciously.

"I'm Jen Burns, Lauren's Mom."

"Oh yeah, hi!"

I start to wheel away, but then stop. "Hey, Christine, can I ask you something?"

She looks startled. "Sure."

"You were Tommy Butler's babysitter, right?" I ask her.

Right away, her eyes well up. I wish I hadn't asked her.

She wipes her tears with her fingers. It takes her a moment to compose herself.

"Yes, I am. Or rather, I was. I loved him so much… I just can't believe that he is gone.

Cringing, I whisper, "Were you there that day?"

Her head shakes no. "No, I wasn't there. I was away in Cape May with my family. Maybe if I was there, this wouldn't have happened to my little guy."

She starts to sob, bending over with her hands on her knees. "What makes it worse is that they're saying Dylan did this to him on purpose. Why would he do that to me?"

Her voice is getting louder. I can't help looking around to see who might be eavesdropping.

I place my hand on her arm. "You can't blame yourself, Christine. I'm sorry for your loss. Take care of yourself."

Hurriedly, I push my grocery cart away. *What the fuck?* I thought she was there that day. I'm sure that I heard Pete ask Dylan where Christine was. If Christine wasn't there, had Pete just gone to work, leaving Tommy home alone? And if so, then why did he ask where she was? And why did Christine say that Dylan did this to *her*? Something isn't right. None of this makes any sense. I *know* I heard Pete ask where Christine was. Maybe there's another Christine?

After putting the groceries away, I sit at my desk and bring up Facebook on my computer, looking for Pete Butler's page. I want to see if there are other friends named Christine in his friend group. I need answers. I want to somehow prove that Dylan didn't mean to kill Pete's kid. The first thing that pops up is Tommy's face. There's a collage of pictures of Tommy at every age. Adorable baby pictures that immediately melt my heart. A picture of him up to bat at t-ball. His sweet face with one baby tooth missing in front.

Tears come to my eyes. I heard this baby die, and I know who did it. Dylan has to pay for this. It's not fair that he's walking the earth while this baby is in the ground.

In the comments under the photos are hundreds of condolence messages from many familiar names, people who I bet hate me now. They write of happy memories of Tommy, of how he brightened the world with his smile.

Sitting back from the screen, I wonder what might have happened if only I had tried to stop Dylan. I could have yelled into the phone. If only I had just screamed at him to stop hurting Tommy, maybe I could have saved this little boy. But I was too ashamed and afraid to get caught listening. Why the fuck did I care about that? I remember thinking that they were just roughhousing, but I'd heard the cries. I didn't know Tommy would end up *dead*. What kind of person does it make me to even consider seeing Dylan again?

Dr. Thorne thought that I might see Dylan as more of a child himself. That I was just taking the role of a protective mother. I'd heard about women who wrote to serial killers in jail, and how they would fall in love and get married. Am I one of those women, desperate enough to keep Dylan in my life at any cost? What if he finds out that I betrayed him by giving a witness statement? Oh my God, I can't take this. I click off of Facebook.

# CHAPTER 16

Tired from all the guilt I'm feeling, I decide to walk Riley to clear my head. I pop on my favorite United Lacrosse baseball cap, even though Lauren always says that I'm trying too hard to be cool when I wear it. After grabbing a doggy poop bag, we head out down Poplar Lane. I enjoy hearing the birds chirping and the wind blowing the leaves in the trees. It's hot out today; I think I heard it was eighty-nine degrees somewhere. The sun warming my body feels healing. I look up, then close my eyes, feeling the rays on my face.

I think about the definition of the word "guilt." The feeling of blameworthiness. For much of my forty-five years, I've rarely felt guilt. I would often listen to my friends talk about all the guilt they felt for not going to the gym, for using a babysitter too much, for not wanting to have sex as much as their husbands did. I never felt that way, even with two divorces under my belt. My first memory of feeling guilt was when I was twelve years old and my grandmother asked me and my sister to come with my dad to visit her on a Sunday night. I had said no, because I wanted to see something on TV. I didn't go, and she died in her sleep that night. The guilt from that has stuck with me all these years. Other than that time, this is the worst experience with guilt I've ever had.

It's half-past four when we get home. Riley pants, searching for her water dish. I find it in the dishwasher. Jack must have washed it. He's good that way. He always picks up after himself and Lauren and me. Lauren's a bit of a slob, but she can't be perfect at everything. I sit down to cool off in the queen's chair.

Startled by my phone, I suddenly wake to find that I've slept for three hours. Ignoring the phone, I run up the stairs to shower. Dylan will be here in thirty minutes. I need to shower, brush my teeth, and blow out my hair. I want him to find me desirable. It's sad, but true.

Dylan arrives on time. He usually just knocks and walks in, but this time is different. Everything is different now. He knocks and waits for me to answer. When I open the door, he's standing a step back from it, with both hands holding up a huge bouquet of wildflowers. I can't help but smile as I let him in. He wraps one arm around me and pulls me in, hugging me while he kisses my face. It reminds me of the first time he kissed me.

I begin, "Hey, how are you?"

Dylan passes the flowers to me. "Okay, I guess, with all that's happened. I've missed talking to you, but I wasn't sure if you wanted to talk to me."

I sigh. "I'm hoping that this all has been a huge misunderstanding."

"I found Tommy passed out," he protests. "I thought he was just asleep."

Christ, he's lying right out of the gate! Needing to stay on track with the plan Kat and I came up with, I bow my head in agreement. I need to make him trust me.

I can't help staring at him. He really is beautiful. No one this good-looking has ever kissed me or told me they liked me. Why *did* he like me? I'm pretty enough for someone handsome who's my age, but someone fifteen years younger doesn't make sense. I guess I had just enjoyed the attention from him so much that I never took note.

Why had he stuck around this long? Maybe he felt like he needed to after I took care of him. Or maybe he needed me for something else. Was I part of something else? Was that it?

He grabs hold of me with one arm and pulls me in again. "Thanks for believing me."

I know I told him I heard him hurt Tommy. I told him that day at the playground. Why is he lying to me? Is he believing his own lies? I stick to the plan.

Hugging him back, I ask, "Do you want a beer?"

He steps back. "I'd love one. Make it two."

We laugh. I get the beers from the fridge and walk past him to the couch in the living room. He sits down at the end of the couch and pulls up his knee.

Handing him a beer, I point to his knee. "Still sore?"

Scratching his knee, he says, "Yes, it aches. And the itchy scar from the incision drives me crazy."

I nod yes. "I remember that from my knee surgery. It goes away eventually."

There I go being motherly, reassuring him that he will get better. Oh, my God, Dr. Thorne was right!

I chug one beer after another while we sit talking about the weather, about Jack's football practices, and what Ivy School Lauren has her mind set on to go to. I'm thankful that the alcohol is making me numb, giving me my favorite kind of courage.

I still want him. I still want those beautiful lips on my body. His sweet smile lights up the room, and I find myself rubbing his calf where it lies next to my hand. I need to convince myself that he still finds me attractive. *Ego*, I think. *This is all about my ego.* I want to prove to myself that I'm pretty enough for someone who looks like him to want me.

"You feel good," I flirt.

Smiling even wider, he says, "Come here."

Trying to appear graceful, I lift myself up from my end of the couch and climb up his legs. Slowly, I press my chest onto his. He leans up and grabs my face with both hands, kissing me. My body tingles with desire. His hands climb up under my shirt, rubbing my back, then scratching it. He grabs at my arms, pulling me in closer. In one swift motion, he pulls my shirt up over my head, then moves his hands to my breasts, breathing heavily. I'm breathing heavily too, but now, suddenly, in fear. I push away from him, adrenaline racing through my veins. I reassure myself that he has stopped.

With his hands up in the air, he asks, "What's up?"

I get up off him, grab my bra and shirt, and walk away into the kitchen. Not looking at him, I answer, "I can't right now. I'm sorry." This annoys me again. Why did I just I just tell him that *I'm* sorry? He should be, for all the bad shit he's brought into my life.

I sit at the kitchen table. Not sticking to the plan, I whisper,

"I heard you, Dylan. I heard you with Tommy. I know that you hurt him. I heard him cry while you hurt him. Why are you lying to me?"

Pissed, Dylan says, "I told you, I wasn't there."

I shake my head. "Dylan, stop! I heard you. You pocket-dialed me. I heard everything. I even heard you say, 'Die, you little shit!'" My hand flies to my mouth.

Dylan gets up from the couch and slowly walks over to me. He puts a hand on the chair back next to me and leans in. "Did you tell anyone that you heard me say that?"

With tears forming, I lie, "No. I protected you. What were you thinking? Why would you kill a kid? He was your friend's boy. I want to understand why you did it. I'll keep protecting you. Just tell me why."

With his head low, he says, "I can't."

"You can't say why?"

"Yes."

He grabs hold of my shoulder, but I jerk away. He looks right into my eyes and kisses my forehead, then walks toward the front door.

I want to tell him to wait, but I'm scared. He needs to go. Relief flows over me when I hear the door close. I jump to lock it behind him. When I get to the door, I see something out of the corner of my eye.

He's still here.

He is leaning against the wall in the dining room. I'm scared that he's planning to hurt me, but then I see his face. He's crying. He wipes his nose on his shirt sleeve, not looking at me.

"Are you alright?" I ask.

He answers, "I had to."

"You had to what?"

He speaks more softly. "He knows."

"Who knows?" I ask, perplexed.

"Pete knows what happened with me and my mom."

He's sobbing so hard, I can't understand what he's saying. I sit him down in the kitchen and get him tissues.

After some time, I ask, "What happened with you and your mom?"

He looks up, red-eyed. "I pushed her and she died."

I jerk away instinctively, horrified. "You killed your mom?"

He is hysterical now. Snot drips all over his shirt. I can't help but to put my hands on his shoulders, trying to console him.

"Babe, you couldn't have meant to kill her, right?" I beg.

He exclaims, "We were fighting about me not working enough. She was saying that I was a waste of space, that I was a bum. As I ran past her, I shoved her. She fell back and hit her head on the foot of the metal coffee table. I killed her. My own mother!"

I try to reassure him. "It was an accident. You should have said it was just an accident."

He continues, "I didn't know what to do except call Pete. I asked him for help. He came over and said that with our rumored volatile history, no one would believe it was an accident. It needed to look like she slipped and hit her head. We lifted her up and placed her on the driveway on the ice. We scooped up as much blood as we could to put under her head. We cleaned up the rest of the blood inside, and then Pete left. He told me to call 911 and say that I found her that way in the driveway. I did as he said."

"And everyone believed it was an accident?"

"Yes!"

Sitting closer to him, I ask, "Is Pete the only one who knows the truth?"

Placing his hands over mine, he pleads, "Yes. Please, Jen, please protect me. Please don't tell anyone what you heard. I love you, Jen."

I put my head down on top of our hands and promise, "I won't tell the police or anyone what I heard. I love you too, Dylan."

I pick up my face and kiss his lips. He has stopped sobbing. I take his hand and lead him back to the couch. Exhausted, he and I lie down, spooning. I pull his arm over me. I turn on the TV, and we quietly snuggle while watching a movie. I just want it to stay like this. Why can't it be this simple? I fall asleep, letting myself believe that he loves me.

# CHAPTER 17

I wake up, stretch, and roll over, only to find that I'm alone on the couch. *Where is he? Where did Dylan go?* The dog is right up in my face.

Getting to my feet is going to be difficult; I have three separate afghans on me. I untangle my legs and stand up. The clock on the Comcast box says 6:00 a.m. I peek around the corner. Dylan is nowhere. I yell, "Dylan, are you here?" No one answers.

Since Kat never sleeps, I pick up my cell to call her.

"Hey, it's Jen."

"I know," Kat grunts.

"Have you had your coffee yet?"

"No, I just got to work. Why are you calling me this early?"

"Dylan slept over, I think, last night."

"What do you mean 'you think?'"

"Well, I just woke up on the couch, and he isn't here."

Kat huffs. "At least you're alive! Did he confess his sins?"

"Kind of."

Kat raises her voice in frustration. "What do you mean 'kind of?'"

"He told me something else, but I can't tell you."

"Really, Jen? Then why are you calling me?"

"I can tell you that we didn't fool around. I freaked out a little. And then I accused him of lying."

"Way to stick to the plan, Jen!"

"He kept saying that he found Tommy that way, that he thought he was sleeping. I couldn't take the lies. After I told him what I knew, he confessed to something else. The thing I can't tell you."

"Okay, okay, I get it. You're still nowhere with why he did it?"

"I didn't say that. One might have to do with the other. I need to investigate. Oh, also, I bumped into Christine. Remember, the girl who was supposed to be babysitting Tommy that day?"

"Yeah, where did you see her?" Kat asks.

"Of all places, the Acme. I almost ran her over with my cart. She was just standing there, staring at the cereal boxes."

"Did you ask her if she was there that day?"

"I'm getting to that!" I say, frustrated. "She said that she was away on a family vacation in the Cape. Isn't that weird?"

"This shit is all weird! What does that tell you, Nancy Drew?"

"From what Dylan told me last night, I think there's a bigger story here. I think maybe Dylan was asked to do what he did to Tommy."

"Christ, Jen, asked by who?"

"I think Pete, Tommy's dad, might be involved somehow."

Kat asks me to hold on. I can hear her talking to Joe, her dad. "Tell Joe I say hi!" I yell into the phone.

"Hi, Jen!" He calls back, hearing me.

Kat gets back on. "Listen, I think you're on to something, but I need to call you back."

"Okay!"

After making myself green tea, I sit at the kitchen table and open my laptop. One of my favorite times of the day is early in the morning when the house is quiet, just me and my dog. I keep looking at my cell for a text from Dylan. You would think he would have left a note.

I pass on the usual Facebook, Snapchat, and Instagram links. I want to go to my online notebook. I need to start keeping track of all these odd things related to Tommy's death. It's passcode guarded, for my eyes only. I decide to number the evidence:

1. Dylan pocket-dials me.
2. Tommy dies while Dylan sits on him.
3. Pete comes home questioning what happened to Tommy.
4. Dylan lies to Pete. Says he found him that way.
5. Dylan killed mom by accident last year.
6. Pete knows Dylan killed his mom.
7. Christine was not babysitting.
8. Christine had a planned vacation with her family.
9. Pete pays a lot of child support to three different women.
10. Pete has more of a motive than Dylan.

Looking at the list, I think I might be getting somewhere. But who kills their own kid? I heard how upset Pete was. He screamed and yelled to call 911. He sounded devastated. But on the other hand, why would Dylan kill Tommy? What could possibly be the reason?

The bigger problem with this theory is that Pete is a cop. No cop is going to accuse another cop, especially one with a dead kid. On the outside, Pete appears to be such a nice person. But people have been known to kill over money. Nancy Grace once said, "I'm on a search for truth!" That's me right now. I don't believe Dylan did this on his own. I remember the last line from a Graham Greene quote, where he says, "One can't love and do nothing."

My cell rings. At first, I think it's Kat calling me back, but it's the number I now associate with Dylan.

"Hey, where did you go?"

"I didn't want to wake you," Dylan answers. "I needed to meet with someone."

"This early?"

"Yeah. Everything is going to be okay."

I couldn't bring myself to ask who he met with… but something tells me it was Pete.

"Do you want to come back for breakfast?" I kind of hate myself for mothering him again.

"No, but thanks, Jen. I'll call you later." His voice sounds sad. I can't help feeling bad for him. For me, the only reason for Dylan killing Tommy is that he was forced to do it.

# CHAPTER 18

My buddy Kev is home from Aruba. I need to get over to his house to see him, and to talk to his mom about all of this. After getting divorced from husband number two, I needed to get a job quick. It was a bad time to be looking for a job in finance. Companies were feeling the down market and letting people go left and right. I had heard Suze Orman, a financial advisor on the radio, recommend finding a job that makes you happy. Working in the financial industry made me miserable. My college education in human resources hadn't prepared me for understanding the stock market. Every time I picked up the phone, I feared not knowing the answer to a question. Where I was sitting, I was supposed to know all the answers. I averaged knowing three out of ten questions asked of me. I tracked it one day. This wasn't to say that I wouldn't find them the answer to their question in the end. I'm very good at follow-up. My boss called me Tenacious Jen because I would never give up until I found an answer.

I took Suze's advice and got a job in child care. Children make me happy. Lori, a teacher, found my resume on Care.com. The rest is history.

I want to surprise my little guy, so I just show up at his house. I know that they're home because Lori's car is in the driveway. With my keys, I open the front door. When Kev sees me, he comes running and jumps right into my arms. He's gotten heavier. I stumble back, laughing.

"I missed you, buddy!" I say, kissing his cheeks.

"I missed you, Jen."

We twirl around and around. Stopping, I put him down and look into his eyes. His skin is brown from the sun, and his hair has turned blonde. Other than my kids, I've never seen a more beautiful child. I would die for this kid.

"Kev, tell me all about Aruba!"

He starts to walk around in a circle, extending his arms. "I fed an iguana some lettuce."

"You did? Did he bite your finger?"

He giggles, "No, Jen. They don't bite."

Raising my eyebrows, I look over at his mom. She shrugs and says, "So I lied a little."

We both laugh. Kevin is oblivious to us. He runs into the playroom to fetch something he wants to show me.

I don't want to ruin the mood, but I make myself ask, "Did you hear about the kid in Tree Lawn who died while you were away?"

"Yes, I saw it on Facebook. Did you know him or his family?"

I sigh. "Yes, it gets worse. Dylan is the young guy I've been seeing."

"The one from your couch?" Lori exclaims.

"Yes, that one."

In a demanding voice says, Lori says, "You're not still seeing him, are you?"

"It's more complicated than that. I'm kind of in cahoots with the Tree Lawn Police."

Ugh. I knew that she would be pissed when she heard I had some involvement in this. Shit, I wish I had stayed home. I know the lecture is coming. Lori is twelve years younger than me, but she's my boss. She pays me to care for her child. The employer-employee relationship can be tricky when it comes to babysitting. You live in their house all day with their kids. It's not like most businesses in the way that more emotion is involved.

I'm stuck on what to say next. It's hard to defend myself for defending a kid-killer. Luckily for me, Kevin comes running back into the room with something in his hand.

"This is for you, Jen-Jen." He hands me a bookmark with a picture of dolphins on it.

I take it from him and hug him tight. "Thank you so much, Kev-buddy. I love it. You know how much I love to read. I'll put it in my book right when I get home."

A big smile comes over his face. "Yay!" He says, jumping up and down.

I stay for a bit longer, but I'm itching to get out of there. I can see Lori texting on her phone with one hand while holding her coffee with the other. She glances my way a few times. I'm sure she must be telling her friends about me and Dylan. Who could blame her? It's sensational news, that her nanny is involved with the guy who killed that kid in Tree Lawn.

I kiss and hug Kevin and wave to Lori while I leave the house. Oh, my God, I need to figure out what really happened that day, before I'm found guilty in the public's eye along with Dylan.

After I'm in the car, my cell rings. It's Lori. She isn't done with me yet. I answer, "Hey, what's up?"

"Jen, what's up is that you have to stay clear of this guy. You can't be seeing him when you're watching my kid."

"Lori, it's more complicated than that. Anyway, I don't start back with you for another few weeks."

"Well this had better be over by then. Jen, I know how much Kev loves you and how great you are with him, but I can't take the chance of this guy being anywhere near my kid."

"I understand. I don't blame you. I'll make sure I'm out of it by September, I promise."

I can hear some relief in her voice when she says, "Good! Be careful, Jen. No man is worth this shit."

"Okay. Bye."

We hang up. I just made a promise that I have to keep. I love Kev as much as I love my own kids. I can't even imagine not being able to see him again. If it's a choice between either Kevin or Dylan, I will always choose Kev. To me, there is no question. I find it funny that it's not the people I trust the most in my life, like my mom, or my ex-husband John, or even Kat, that have made me see the light. It's the love I have for a four-year-old boy that has given me perspective on my situation. I have the next few weeks to figure this out. If I don't, I will break ties with Dylan.

## CHAPTER 19

"Go to bed. Tomorrow will be a better day!"

Words to live by, from my dad. Once, I had a few bad weeks in college, and was feeling very low. Not suicidal, but it felt like I was heading that way. I called my dad at work. Rarely did I speak to my dad; Mom was my confidant, first and foremost, though, if I had a financial question, my mom would pass the phone to my father. That day, though, I needed more than my mom's gentle compassion and understanding. It seemed more serious. I was having thoughts of leaving this planet.

I had picked up the phone and called my dad at work. His secretary answered. She could hear me crying, and told me to hold on while she got him out of a meeting.

He was quick to pick up the line. "What's up, honey? Everything okay?"

A full sob broke loose. It took me a minute to get myself together.

"Dad, I'm not doing well. I feel anxious and overwhelmed. I don't think I can do this anymore."

I didn't expect him to ask questions. In my experience, men

don't want details.

"Honey, go to bed right now," he had answered. "Close your eyes, and I promise tomorrow will be a better day."

I had thought to myself, *That's all he's got for me? Those are his words of wisdom?*
Nevertheless, I decided to listen to him that day. It wasn't even dark outside yet, but I washed my tears from my face, brushed my teeth, and went straight to bed. I remember lying there thinking that one good night of sleep couldn't be the answer, but when I woke in the morning, I felt much better. He had been right—it was crazy, but true. Maybe it was because I believed and trusted him that my mind just got better. I don't know, but to this day I try to go to bed early when life gets shitty.

I'm thinking tonight will be one of those nights. As soon as the sun goes down, I'm hitting the sack.

But right now, I need to get busy on the laptop. My involvement in this has made me feel like I'm in danger. I don't have any specific reason to think that it might not end well for me, it's just a gut feeling. My friends think that I've got a sixth sense. For years, I've predicted both big and small events before they happen. I think it's more like premonition, or good intuition. I could really use some of those abilities right now, to figure out this mystery.

Before I realize it, I'm sitting there staring at Pete Butler's Facebook page. Trying not to focus on Tommy's pictures, I go to his friends listing. I type "Christine" in the search box. Up come four women named Christine. I click on each of their pages. Two are private, so I can't see their profiles. Another Christine is the girl I spoke with in the Acme, while the final Christine is one who lives out of state. The private profiles show pictures of kids. They wouldn't be babysitting Pete's kid if they're busy with their own.

I focus in on the original Christine, from the Acme. I pull up her page and click on her photos. There are lots of junior prom pictures. The dresses these girls wear, dear God. Not even now do I show that much cleavage.

In the pictures, Christine's hair is much lighter than she wears it now, and she has several braids holding it back off her face. The dress she is wearing is draped on her and tied up on one shoulder. She looks gorgeous.

There are also pictures of her with family. My laptop has a touch screen, so I use my finger to scroll through the rest of her pictures. There are a few selfies with Tommy. I figure when she was babysitting, but, then my finger lands on a picture that stuns me. It's a picture of Christine with Dylan. He has his arm around her waist. They both have great big smiles. My heart stops as suddenly as if it's been hit by a bolt of electricity. *What are they doing together?* A tiny, nagging, jealous voice in the back of my head surfaces, whispering that they actually make a pretty attractive pair. Oh, my God, how could I ever compete with her? What am I saying? She isn't even eighteen yet! Has he been seeing her while we've been together? Maybe there is nothing to it. They could be just friends. Even though I know well enough that men and women can't be 'just friends' unless one is gay.

I find a few more pictures of Christine and Dylan in group shots. None are as intimate as the one with his arm around her. My heart is sinking. I log off of Facebook and log into my online notebook. Reluctantly, I add to my evidence list:

11. Possible sexual relationship between Dylan and Christine?

I hit save and make sure to log out of my notebook. I close the laptop and decide it's time to eat. These days, I find myself missing too many meals. I don't eat when I'm stressed out. After seeing that picture of Dylan and Christine I need some comfort food. I go to the kitchen to make some mac and cheese.

# CHAPTER 20

It's a new day. I had gone to bed really early last night. I look at my cell to see if anyone has texted me during my hibernation, and see three messages from Dylan's new number and five messages from Kat's number.

Needing amusement, I open Kat's texts first.

*Where are you?*

*You're not answering your cell, bitch!*

*I'm calling the cops if you don't get back to me soon.*

*Did shithead mistake you for a kid and smother your ass? Seriously, Jen. Call me back!*

I text her back: *It's Jen from the great beyond……*

My cell rings. It's Kat.

I answer, "Yo-yo!"

"Where the hell were you last night?" Kat screams. "You scared the shit out of me!"

"Jesus, Kat, relax!"

"Don't tell me to relax! You're dating a killer, and I'm supposed to relax? Really, where were you?"

Yawning, I say, "Sleeping. Alone!"

"All night?"

"Yes, all night."

"Well, text me the next time you plan to sleep all night. You gave me a heart attack!"

"Why didn't you just come over?" I ask. "You know where I hide the house key."

"I thought about it. But, number one, I was drunk, and number two, if Dylan was in the process of killing you, I didn't want him to get my ass, too."

"Funny, Kat! I was stalking Christine, the babysitter, on Facebook, and found something interesting."

Kat mocks, "Okay, Nancy Drew, what did you find out?"

"I was browsing her photos and found a picture of her with Dylan."

"Hmm. Interesting, but you know Dylan practically lived on Pete's couch. The picture could have been taken at one of Pete's many parties."

"Maybe, but he had his arm around her, and she was right up there next to him. It was dated last year. Christine was barely seventeen in the picture. You should have seen it. They looked pretty cozy." I'm not able to keep the hint of jealousy out of my voice.

"You think this is another piece of the puzzle?"

"Christine had an all-access pass to Tommy. Christine has some kind of relationship with Dylan. Dylan killed Tommy. Something is there, right?" I question Kat.

Kat grunts, "As usual, Miss 'There's-No-Such-Thing-as-Coincidence,' though you might be right. Now, what's your plan?"

"I need to see Dylan again, hopefully tonight."

Kat, knowing me too well, says, "Don't get nonsensical and jealous with him about Christine. Just stay cool and find out some more answers, like why he fucking killed Tommy."

"Yes, *Mother.*"

We hang up. I look to see what Dylan texted me last night. His messages have an angry tone, and are followed by many question marks. He demands to know if I'm dodging his calls. Part of me is happy that he's showing concern, but I'm confused by his possessiveness.

I text him back, explaining that I was tired, so I went to bed early. Then I ask if he wants to meet at our first date place. I'm still using code, remembering that my cell is bugged.

*Sure,* he texts back. *What time?*

*8 p.m.*, I respond.

I'm about to run up the stairs to shower, but then I see John's car parked out front. Opening the door, I'm startled to see John standing right in front of me. We both yell in surprise. Laughing, I back up to let him in. He isn't laughing.

He walks into the kitchen and sits at the table.

"This is some of the evidence they have against Dylan. I need to go over it with you. Sit."

"Okay." I sit down in front of him.

He lays out what looks to me like a PowerPoint presentation. This makes me giggle a little.

"This is not funny, Jennifer!"

Does this guy think we are still married?

"I have written out the types of evidence the Tree Lawn Police have collected thus far."

"Are you supposed to be showing me this?"

"No. Please just look at it, Jen."

"Okay, okay!" I say, looking down at the paper.

**Physical Evidence**: DNA from room, couch, and their clothing. Skin from under Tommy's fingernails. Liquid found on pillows. Fingerprints. Bruising of the skin. Hair follicles.

**Demonstrative Evidence**: No motive yet. The police think Dylan was roughhousing with Tommy and just snapped and killed him by asphyxiation.

**Testimonial Evidence**: You and Pete Butler

"Okay, I get it, John!"

"You're my kids' mother. I don't like what people are saying about you."

"What are they saying?" I wave my hand at him. "Forget it. I don't want to know. John, I'm giving myself until September to find out what really happened that day. Dylan killing Tommy does not make any sense. It could have been revenge, but I've never heard Dylan say a bad word about Pete. It could have been done to keep a secret." I immediately regret what I have said to John.

"It could have been over money, but neither Dylan or Pete has a ton of money."

"It could have been about sex or jealousy." The picture of Dylan with his arm around Christine comes to mind. Could that really have something to do with this?

"Please give me some time. Dropping this now would leave me believing that I brought a man into this house that gets pleasure from killing kids. I can't live with that. I need to know why."

John says, "Okay!" He grabs his papers up and heads towards the door.

I run after him and grab his arm.

"John, are you okay?"

"Yes, I just hope you know what you're doing."

"Just until September, I promise," I say.

He nods and goes out the door.

# CHAPTER 21

What's next? My life feels like a giant game of dodgeball.

Riley is staring at me. She wants to go for a run. I change into running clothes and head out with the only one who doesn't judge me, my dog.

Today we run toward Red Bank, a cool town full of young, hip people who could care less about what's happening in the upscale neighborhood next door. It feels more like October than the end of August. The air is cool and crisp. I love running when it's cold, and even more so when it rains.

We turn the corner, and I can see the street Kat lives off of. She will be at work by now.

When John and I bought the land in Tree Lawn, we were excited to build our dream home. John had grown up in Tree Lawn, and wanted to stay there. He loved the idea of small-town living, where our future kids could walk to school. At first, I loved the idea as well, but it soon became clear that I wasn't like the other women in town. I didn't care about having fancy things, or whether they had fancy things. My favorite shoes were my running sneakers. I found that I would like them individually, but as a group, they all became too competitive. Whoever didn't make it to a gathering would fall victim to their petty criticism. When it came to people in my life, my motto was "friends to the end," even with my ex-husbands. I rarely spoke ill of my true friends. I found it to be a waste of my time to sit around gossiping about whoever wasn't there. Soon after I bailed out of this group of women, I heard that a rumor had been started that John was having an affair with a young, pretty client of his. These women were ruthless. I never went back. The funny thing is that I get along fine with their daughters, who are Lauren's age. They're more my friends than their mothers were. I heard that these same women now refer to me as "crazy" or "wacky." That doesn't bug me, because I think there's some truth to it. In college, I was never even comfortable pledging a sorority. I was afraid that I might get trapped in a group of people who didn't understand me, or wanted to control how I lived or who I associated with.

I've lived in Tree Lawn for twenty years now, and still haven't made many friends. I did befriend my neighbor Vanessa. She's cool, and we don't ask much of each other. We keep each other at arm's length, asking for a stick of butter or a cup of sugar. She's an easy friend to have. Often, early in the morning, we would stand on our back porches, drinking our coffee and talking about what our kids were up to, and she would listen to me complain about all my husbands. She still laughs hard at all my stories. Come to think of it, we haven't had a conversation about what happened yet. I hope she won't get too upset with me.

Riley and I get caught up on a stop sign pole. She's gone one way, and me the other. I untangle us, and we head toward the main street in Red Bank. It's still early enough that we can run on the sidewalk in front of the stores. We pass a fancy women's clothing store where only very pretty girls get hired to work. This gets me thinking about Christine. She is a real beauty! I know that there is something between them. Why wouldn't he want to be with her? Also, these kids are much more advanced sexually then we were thirty years ago. I was a virgin until senior year in high school and I had dated my boyfriend at the time a year before we did it. From what I've heard, the average age for a girl's first sexual experience these days is way younger. How am I going to be able to see Dylan and not ask him if he dated her? Her age also makes it weird for me to ask. I'm not going to say anything. He has enough accusations being thrown at him right now.

When we get to the end of my street, I can see a police car parked in front of my house. Jesus, I thought they were keeping a lid on my involvement in this case. I run up to his window. He's not a very alert cop, because I need to knock on the window to get his attention.

It's the same guy who interviewed me at the station.

"What are you doing here?" I ask suspiciously.

"Hello, Jen. We're concerned that not much conversation is happening between you and Dylan on your phone. You know the plan behind bugging your phone is that we can get him to incriminate himself, right?"

"Yeah, I get that, but I can't be too obvious about it. I'm working on it."

Rolling his eyes, he asks, "How are you working on it?"

"Well, I've got some theories—"

He interrupts me, "That's our job, Jen. But can you tell me what these theories are?"

Ignoring his question, I ask, "How is Pete Butler doing?"

"How do you think, Jen? He's devastated. He had to take a leave of absence."

Riley starts to pull me to the front door, and I let her.

I yell back at him, "As soon as I reach my verdict, you'll be the first to know!" I give him a big, toothy smile. He nods his head back at me, but doesn't smile in return.

Welcome to the 'I-hate-Jen' list.

# CHAPTER 22

Dylan has been texting me all day. He has asked a few times if I'm still meeting him at the bar tonight. I finally texted him back that I 'will most definitely be there.' I need to tell Kat my plans for tonight, but I hate to bug her at work. I text her to call me when she has a moment.

Right away, she calls me. "What's up, crazy?"

"Dylan is acting weird about meeting up tonight," I answer.

"Weird like, he-plans-to-kill-you weird?"

"Maybe." I swallow loudly.

"Jesus, Jen, then don't meet him."

"But I need to find out somehow if there's something between him and Christine. I want to see his reaction when I bring up her name. Christine said something in the Acme that made me think."

"What did she say?"

"She said, 'Why did Dylan do this to me?' Not to Tommy, to her. I think that's a strange thing to say."

"Jen, normally I would say you're overthinking this, but I

have to admit, that's weird. Although, kids these days only think of themselves. Maybe she's only seeing Tommy's death in terms of how it affects her."

"No, she seemed to be genuinely upset about missing Tommy."

"How do you plan to bring up her name? Wait, forget that question. I know you'll find a way. Just don't be too obvious. Also, don't drink too much and get all emotional, okay?"

"Okay. We're meeting where we had our first date with you and Scott. Do you remember? I think meeting him at a public bar is safer than alone at my house."

"The bar that's in the basement of that house?"

"Yes."

"Let me get this straight: you're meeting your lover-slash-kid-killer in the dark basement of an old house at night?"

"Sounds about right."

"Jen, you're one dumb-ass bitch!"

We both start laughing.

"Don't shave your legs or your bush, and wear those granny panties you have. Then you're guaranteed to go home alone. If you don't report in every fifteen minutes, I'll go there and drag you out by your hair. You got that?"

"Yes, Mother!"

I'm missing my kids being here. I text Lauren to see if she wants to go for ice cream.

She says yes, and to come pick her up at the high school, where she's helping with freshman orientation.

When I get there, Lauren is standing out front, talking to some boys in their football uniforms. Jack must be here at practice, too. Seeing me, she waves and comes running, her high ponytail bouncing up and down. Admiring her beauty never gets old.

"Hey, girl. How was orientation?"

"Mom, they're so cute," she says, with a big toothy smile.

"Did you see Jack at practice?"

"Yes, he gave me a nod earlier. He thinks he's cool!"

"Lauren, he *is* cool!"

We laugh. Jack is handsome, like his dad. He's quiet most of the time, but his one-liners can make us die laughing. He has a very dry sense of humor. He got that from his dad as well.

Lauren and I both get chocolate cones and head outside to sit.

"Lauren, I need a favor. I need you to ask Christine for her cell phone number."

Lauren moans. "Mom, I'm not really friends with her. That'll be awkward."

"That's why I called it a favor."

"Fine. What do you want to talk to her about?"

"Now don't overreact, Lauren, but I think there's some kind of relationship between Dylan and Christine."

She makes a disgusted face. "He's like, old, mom. Why would Christine want to date *him*?"

"I'm not sure, Lauren. That's why I need to talk to her."

"Okay, I'll message her on Facebook now."

These days, technology makes life happen much faster. Christine answers Lauren right back, and gives her the cell number without much thought. Maybe she has something to say to me too. I can't wait to talk to her, but I decide to see Dylan first and call her in the morning.

## CHAPTER 23

My mood is somber while I primp to meet with Dylan. I used to jack up the music and dance around and sing when getting ready for a date with him, but tonight I don't feel like singing. I find those big panties Kat was talking about in the back of a drawer. They ride up on my stomach. I tuck them into the waistband of my jeans. Kat is right: there's no way I would let him see these on me.

I want to beat him there, so I arrive twenty minutes early and park. I don't go in. I want to see him arrive. A car pulls up, and he waves from the passenger seat to someone driving. I can't see who it is, and I don't recognize the car. I suddenly realize that I really don't know much about Dylan, such as where he's staying these days now that he can't stay at Pete's house. Maybe he's hooked up with another older woman, so he has somewhere to sleep at night. These thoughts don't help my mood.

He walks down the driveway and into the bar. He hasn't seen me waiting. I take a moment to breathe. I'm losing that loving feeling for him. It was fun with him for all those months, being fancy-free. But now this feels like a chore.

It's a lot of work to find out why your so-called boyfriend killed a little kid.

I make myself get out of the car, and start walking towards the door. I've just about reached it when Dylan comes popping out.

He has his phone raised up. "I was just calling you," he states.

"Why? I'm not late, am I?"

"No, just worried you wouldn't show."

"Dylan, I told you I was coming. Here I am. Let's get a drink."

He follows me back inside. No kiss. No hug. Things are not as they were. Why do I care? I know that this relationship has an end date of August 31. He's calling me "baby" and rubbing my back, but I don't recognize this guy. He's trying too hard to please me, and it's coming off as disingenuous.

"What did you do today?" I ask.

"I met with my court-appointed lawyer. He thinks the case will be dropped because of lack of evidence. He said that because I routinely sleep on Pete's couch, the DNA from the couch pillows doesn't prove anything."

"What about my witness statement?"

I can't believe I just asked him that.

He doesn't even flinch. "What you told them isn't enough to convict me with."

With that, he leans in and kisses my cheek, as if to say "thanks." Now I'm pissed. Because of what I didn't say on my witness statement, he isn't going to court. How did I become judge and jury?

"That's good, Dylan. I hope that for your sake, your lawyer's right."

The bartender keeps feeding us beers. He doesn't seem to recognize Dylan, which makes it easier. Dylan tells me that the restaurant fired him after he was arrested, and that he's looking for work in construction. He says that the further he goes away from Tree Lawn, the less they seem to know about "what happened." Dylan using those words to describe the murder of his friend's son makes my blood boil.

Feeling a little tipsy, I decide to pry. "What's with you and Christine?"

His head flicks a bit when he hears her name.

"We're friends. I met her at Pete's house. She was Tommy's sitter. She was there with Tommy all the time, even when she wasn't working. Why do you ask?"

Shit, I didn't think ahead. "I was on Facebook and I saw a picture of you two together."

He looks down and away. I knew it! There's something there.

"She has some kind of crush on me, so I'm nice to her."

I lift my beer to toast him. "I can't blame her for that." I look straight ahead. I feel like he will figure out that I know the truth. I finish my beer and ask the bartender for another one.

Dylan leans in and whispers in my ear. "I miss you, Jen."

Damn, he's cute. *Cute,* I remind myself. *Like a child. Because he is one.*

I drop the subject of Christine, and we talk about the news.

We laugh and kiss and drink a lot.

The later it gets, the more panicked I feel. I need to get myself home without him tagging along. Someone dropped him off. He doesn't have a car. Obviously, he thinks he's going home with me. Luckily, I can't drive because I've had too much to drink. I need Kat.

I text her, *I need you to show up here and then drive me home. I can't figure out how to ditch him. He will want to come home with me.*

Kat texts right back, *Be there in ten.*

Yes, I'm safe! Dylan is unaware that Kat is on her way. When she gets here, I'll act surprised. Kat will say that I'm too drunk, and that she'll take me home. We've done this before, when I needed saving from all the bad dates I met on Match.com. Dylan can't rebut by saying that he will drive me home, because he has no car. I start to relax and enjoy my alcohol.

Kat walks in, looking right at me, and says, "There you are! Why aren't you answering your texts, girl?"

"Hey, Kat!" I move in for a big hug, and whisper in her ear, "Thank you."

Dylan's face is humorless. He is *not* happy to see Kat. He doesn't like that she has interrupted his evening. But I do. She points at me. "Dylan, do you mind if I take this drunk-ass home?"

I put my arm around her shoulder and laugh out loud. Maybe I'm putting on too big of a drunk-girl show, but Dylan nods at her, and off we go out the door.

"Damn, girl," Kat asks. "You really that drunk?"

I straighten up. "Of course not, I just played along."

Kat laughs. "Girl, you're good! What happened? What did you find out?"

"Dylan thinks he's off the hook for Tommy's murder. Not enough evidence. He also said that Christine is the one who has feelings for him, but I don't believe him."

I put my arm back over Kat's shoulder. "Thanks again, friend, for coming to my rescue!"

Kat pats me on my stomach. "What are friends for?"

We climb into Kat's extremely clean car. I try not to touch anything.

"You better not puke in my car, jackass!"

I put my hand to my mouth and pretend to gag. "Not funny, Jen," she says, "You know I'll be the one to kill you if you throw up in my Lexus."

*Bing!* A text from Dylan. *We're good, right?*

"Kat, he wants to know if we're good. Is he fucking *kidding* me? I'm such an ass to have stuck with him this long. This motherfucker is having sex with young girls. He's practically a pedophile. He likes them young, so he can control them. I'm such a fucking pushover. I nursed him back to health for a month; I bathed him, fed him, did his fucking laundry. Ugh, I'm fucking *pathetic*."

"Kat, easy girl. You're not the one who killed a kid."

"Good point, but I'm still the one protecting him."

In sync, her brows rise. "How are you protecting him?"

"I didn't tell the police everything."

"What? What haven't you told me, bitch?"

"He said something bad to Tommy, worse than what I said. He told Tommy to die!"

"What the fuck, Jen? That proves he was trying to kill him!"

"I know." I cover my head with my hands.

Kat exclaims, "You need to tell John and ask him what to do."

We get to my house. I need to sleep. My head is already starting to hurt.

"Drink some water and take some Tylenol, dumbass. Love you!"

"Bye, Kat. Thanks again!"

# CHAPTER 24

I wake with a terrible head ache. As I've aged, my tolerance for alcohol has decreased. No way can I go for a run.

After taking the dog out, I sit down at my computer. I want to be ready to ask Christine some questions. I know she'll say nothing happened at first, but I'll convince her to trust me. If I tell her the whole truth of what I heard Dylan say to Tommy, she'll want to tell me her truth.

I pace in the kitchen for the next two hours. It's still too early to call her. Finally, it's 9 a.m. I dial her number. She answers on the fifth ring.

With a squeaky voice she says, "Hello?"

"Hey, Christine, this is Lauren's mom again. Can you talk?"

"Hold on." I hear her close her door. "Hey, Mrs. Burns."

"Oh please, call me Jen. Christine, I need to ask you some personal questions. I won't tell a soul."

"I think I know what this is about." There's a pause. "Dylan?"

"Yes. I just want to know why he would kill Tommy."

"Jen, I can't really tell you."

"Please, Christine! If I tell you what I heard Dylan say that day, when he was roughhousing with Tommy on the couch, will you trust me then?"

"Okay, what did you hear?"

"I heard him say, 'Die, Tommy!'"

I hear the phone drop. She's crying; I can hear sobbing.

"Christine! Christine?"

She picks up the phone and says, "He did this because of me!"

"What? Why?"

"He became controlling. He wanted to know where I was all the time. If I told him I was going to my friend's house, I would catch him spying near their house. He didn't like me hanging out with my friends."

"Are you telling me that he stalked you?"

"Yes. But after his accident, when he was living with you, he only texted me."

I breathe in hard, and hold it in silence. *Oh my God, while I was taking care of his sorry ass, he was obsessing over her.* Breathe.

"Please tell me what makes you think that he killed Tommy because of you."

"He was oddly jealous of how much I loved Tommy. He would say that he wasn't my kid, or stomp off when I cuddled with Tommy. He was so weird about it. He was jealous of a *five-year-old boy.*" She starts to cry again.

"Were there any signs that he could be abusive?"

"Yes. He broke two of my cell phones. The first time, he thought I was texting another guy. He took my cell and smashed it down, shattering the front screen. The second time he took my phone, he grinded it into the cement sidewalk. At first, I felt like he must really love me, to have such a bad reaction, but after it happened again, I became scared of him and broke things off."

"And he continued to contact you?"

"Yes, he still texts me. Some texts say how much he loves me, but others threaten the people I love. That's how I know he killed Tommy because of me."

"Does Pete know that you two were in a relationship?"

"No, we kept it hidden because of my age. Only my best friend, Sarah, knows."

"Christine, you need to tell the police about his threats. This gives them his motive!"

"Jen, I can't. It's too embarrassing. He's a lot older than I am, so he'll get arrested for that too. I know I shouldn't care what happens to him, but I do."

"Believe me, I get that. This is a lot to put on yourself. I haven't even told the police the whole truth. Maybe we can go together."

"You would do that? Even though you know that he's been texting me while you were together?"

"Fuck him, Christine! I'm going to call Lauren's dad and ask him to set up a meeting at the police station. In the meantime, you need to tell your parents all of this. They might want to take you to the police themselves. Don't worry, Christine, they love you. You'll get through this."

Christine agrees by saying, "Okay."

I hang up, hoping her parents will understand.

# CHAPTER 25

I think I hear a knock at the front door, and push back my chair. I look out the dining room window to see John standing there. He beat me to it. When I start to open the door, he pushes by me.

"Jen, you're not going to believe what happened."

Whatever it is, he doesn't seem to be mad at me. He sits down on top of the kitchen table. I lean against the pantry with one foot up, bracing myself.

"What is it, John?"

"Pete Butler went to the police station last night to admit to a crime."

I gasp. "He had something to do with Tommy's death?"

"No, he says he helped destroy evidence that might have implicated Dylan in another crime."

"Don't tell me, when he killed his mother?"

"What the fuck, Jen? You knew about this?"

I fold my arms in front of my body. "Yes, calm down. He convinced me that it was an accident."

"Well, Pete says that Dylan shoved his mom, which caused

her to fall backwards, leading to her death. Dylan called Pete for help, and they both covered up what really happened."

I guess this means Pete Butler had nothing to do with Tommy's death. It was all Dylan's doing.

"Is Pete in trouble now?"

"Yes, they've reopened that case, and Pete has been suspended indefinitely. Pete said that he was coming clean now because he can't take the guilt of knowing that Dylan had killed before. He says that helping Dylan cover up that crime led to his own son's death. Can you be done with this asshole now?"

"Yes, yes."

John starts for the door. I want to tell him about Christine and Dylan, and the stalking, and the threats he made to her, but I can't. I'm ashamed of myself. Everyone had been right. Dylan was just using me. I'm such a fool.

After he leaves, I decide to toughen up and go to the police myself. I'll tell them what I left out of my witness statement, and my theory on Dylan's motive behind killing Tommy. Of course, what I tell them won't matter unless Christine tells the police herself.

All showered, I head over to the Tree Lawn police station. I tell myself to just keep moving. This time, when I walk in, all eyes are on me. It seems like the whole police force is in the station. I can't help thinking how much Kat would love seeing all these men in uniforms, but remind myself to focus as I walk up to the front desk.

"Can I speak to whomever is in charge of the Tommy Butler case?"

I hadn't caught the name of the officer who questioned me. A young cop asks me to follow him, and brings me back to the room where I had the witness interview. I sit down, and he shuts the door behind him. There's a dark window in the room. and I know that the other cops must be looking at me and saying nasty things. In comes the same cop. He puts out his hand to shake mine officially. "This is Sergeant McDonald," says the first cop.

Kat would love this. "What was your name again?"

"Sergeant McDonald."

"As in Ronald?" I ask him. I hear laughter outside the darkened window. I had asked knowing it would expose them all for gawking.

"Yes, how can I help you?" the sergeant asks.

I tap the mic. "Is this turned on?"

"Yes, it's recording our conversation."

"Okay. As you know, my name is Jennifer Burns. I'm here to add to the first witness statement I made about the murder of Tommy Butler. As I previously told you, Dylan pocket-dialed me while he was, as I thought, roughhousing with Tommy Butler. I overheard Dylan teasing Tommy about crying. I heard Dylan ask if what he was doing hurt Tommy."

I start to cry. Sergeant McDonald puts one finger up to say stop. "I'll be right back." He says, leaving the room, and immediately returns with a box of tissues for me. He waves his hand for me to continue.

"Okay, where was I?"

"You had just finished saying that Dylan asked Tommy if

what he was doing hurt him."

*Big breath in.* "This is the part I omitted. Dylan said to Tommy, 'Die, you little shit!'"

I heard men gasp outside the window. Sergeant McDonald doesn't react at all. He sits back in his chair and smiles.

"Why didn't you tell us this the first time, Ms. Burns?"

"I was protecting him. I know now that I shouldn't have."

"After what Christine told you?"

"How do you know about that?"

He points at my phone.

"Oh, that's right. I understand. Have you spoken to Christine yet?"

"I can't tell you that, but what I can tell you is that we now have enough evidence to prosecute Dylan Jagger, thanks to you. Officers are searching for him right now, to bring him in for additional questioning."

My head pops up. "Did you just thank me?"

"Yes. We knew nothing about his relationship with Tommy's babysitter, Christine. You did a very good investigative job for us, so thank you. But now it's in your best interest to stop seeing Dylan Jagger."

"No problem!"

As I leave the police station, I think about how happy John will be with me, and how the kids can come back to my house now. I'm too exhausted to end it with Dylan today, even though it never really started. I'll call him tomorrow on my cell; then the police can hear me break ties with him.

CHAPTER 26

My plan for the night is to rent a movie on demand and chill out. There's no way I can muster up enough energy to go for a run, but some fresh air might help me feel better. I grab the leash and head out with Riley. The air is still chilly, with not a cloud in the sky. The sun warms my body and helps heal my soul. I know that Sergeant McDonald said that it's not a time for my self-pity, but when Dylan goes on trial, everyone will know how pathetic I am. All those Tree Lawn moms are going to have a party with this. Thank God I never sent Dylan a naked selfie.

I feel like I'm in mourning over someone's death. This entire relationship with Dylan was all in my head. My friends and family tried to warn me, but I didn't listen. I feel burned. He played me. I'm stupid for believing he cared for me. *No more men,* I pledge to myself.

The world outside seems less hostile. Maybe word is getting out that I saved the day.

Through my own jealousy, I had figured out the secret relationship between Christine and Dylan. I'm still shocked. I never saw this abusive side of Dylan.

My cell rings, and I see that it's Kat. I don't know if I can face her ridicule right now, but after the ninth ring, I answer.

"What's up, Kat?"

"'What's up, Kat?' What's up with you? You don't sound well. I bet your head is killing you today, after last night's pops." She laughs.

"I can't right now, Kat. Can I talk to you later?"

"Sure, Jen. I'm sorry. But don't forget to call me later, okay?"

"Yup."

Riley is sniffing all over the place. She pulls me up to someone with big black boots on. I look up, and it's Pete Butler. I don't know how he got there. I didn't see him coming. He must have gone to the house, seen my car there, and assumed I was out walking the dog.

Startled, I step back. He walks toward me with his arms extended. Riley gives him a bit of a growl, making Pete step back and puts his hands up.

"Riley, I'm trying to hug your mom here. Easy, girl."

He looks terrible. Unshaven and gray. His eyes are bloodshot. I'm hoping it's from crying and not from being drunk. I still don't move or say anything.

He puts his hands up again. "Jennifer, can I hug you?"

I step forward, and he grabs hold of me. It's the tightest hug he's ever given me.

"Thanks, Jen, for helping me get him. I can hardly live with myself. I let him into our lives. I knew he had killed his own mother. Please, forgive me, Jen. Please?" He's crying so hard, his body is shaking.

I say, "I forgive you, Pete. You weren't the only one tricked by him. He lived on my couch for over a month while I nursed him back to health. I thought I was doing the right thing, because he had no parents."

"But you didn't know then that he had killed his mother, like I did!"

I step back to look him in the eyes.

"We were all duped by him. What he did to Tommy wasn't your fault. Who would think he had it in him to hurt a child? Look where we live. Things like that don't happen around here. Please don't blame yourself, Pete."

"Thanks, Jen. And thanks for helping my squad nail his ass. I wouldn't be able to live knowing he was walking the streets free."

"I'm glad I could help."

He walks off towards his car with his head hanging low. I feel sorry for him. The only thing Dylan hurt me with were my feelings. After seeing Pete, I know I need to get over myself. At least I got out of this unscathed.

I can't wait to just lie down in my queen's chair. When I get home, I pick up Riley's bowl to fill it with water. My hands shake as I try to hold the bowl still under the faucet. This has been physically and mentally exhausting. I need to sit still and not think about any of it. I climb into my chair and pull an afghan over me. Time for rest.

# CHAPTER 27

My slumber is interrupted by a banging on the sliding glass door by the kitchen. I look up and see Dylan standing outside with his hands on his hips. I walk up to the door and make sure it's locked, not getting too close.

I yell through the glass, "Dylan, the police are looking for you."

"I know, my lawyer told me," he yells back. "I'm going to the station after I talk to you."

"What do you want?"

Dylan puts his arms up to touch the door. "I want to hold you."

"Dylan, are you fucking kidding me? I hate you! You fucking liar!"

He lowers his voice. "Jen, what are you talking about? You love me. You promised to protect me."

I take a step. "I spoke to Christine. I know everything. You're a fucking sociopath!"

"Christine lied to you. There is nothing between us."

"Yes, I know that! You're stalking her!"

"No, she's lying! I broke it off with her months ago."

I step even closer to the window. "You killed little Tommy because she rejected you, you fucking jealous *psychopath*."

Dylan slams both of his fists on the glass. His eyes are slits. His lips are tensed. He looks like he might explode. I run for my cell phone, then hold it up so he can see that I've dialed 911.

He screams, "You fucking cunt! I never loved you. You were just an easy lay. I'll kill you, too!" Then he's gone.

I run to the front door to make sure it's locked, then search to see if all the windows are locked too. My hands are shaking as I put the phone to my ear.

"911. What's your emergency?"

"Yes, Dylan Jagger is here threatening to kill me."

"Is he inside your house?"

"No, he's outside. I can't see him now. Please send someone soon. I don't know if he's still out there."

Within minutes, the two Tree Lawn police cars are outside. Three officers run around the house while Sergeant McDonald walks to the front porch. I open the door before he knocks.

"Hi, Sergeant McDonald. Thanks for coming this fast."

"Is he in the house?"

"No, I never let him in. He screamed at me through the kitchen slider." I point to the door.

"Well, that's a good thing. His lawyer knows about Peter Butler coming in to confess to the cover-up of Dylan's mom's death."

I ask, "Has Christine come in yet?"

"Yes, she and her parents are at the station now. After this call came in, we asked them to stay until Dylan is picked up."

Meekly, I say, "I told him that I had spoken with Christine, and that he was a lying psychopath who killed Tommy for revenge."

McDonald smirks and says, "That's about right."

"Dylan threatened to kill me too!"

McDonald nods. "That alone can get him five years of imprisonment. Come with us to the station to make a formal statement."

I ask them to wait a minute for me. I need to change into sweats and find my purse.

When I come back out, all but McDonald are back in their squad cars.

"They're going to search the neighborhood for any sign of Dylan," McDonald says. "Don't worry, we'll get him."

He goes to open the back door of the patrol car for me, but I shake my head. "No."

He laughs and moves to the front, opening that door for me. "Okay, get in."

He's cute. I can't help wondering if he's single.

At the station, I don't see Christine or her parents. I assume that they're in the room where I was interviewed. McDonald shows me to his desk, and I take a seat. He walks away in the direction of the interview room. A few minutes later, he comes back.

"Okay, Christine and her parents are being interviewed. They brought their lawyer."

"Do I need John to be here?"

"No, you don't need him to make a complaint."

That's a relief. I don't want to tell John that Dylan came to the house and threatened to kill me. If he knows that, he won't let the kids stay at my house.

He asks me again what Dylan Jagger had threatened to do to me. This time, I add the fact that he punched the glass with his fists while he said it.

"What do I do if he starts to harass me?"

"You can get a protective order by the court."

"Come on, Sergeant, like that'll keep this kid away?"

"I get it, but that would be the next action for you to take. Here, this is my cell number. Call me if you feel threatened again."

"Thanks." Blushing, I plug the numbers into my cell phone.

I sign whatever it is he puts in front of me. At this point, I trust him.

He walks off again with the paperwork. An hour goes by before he returns this time.

"Listen, Sarge, can I get out of here?"

"I don't want you to go until I hear that we have Dylan in custody, alright?"

I let out a big sigh. "I'm stuck here?"

He bobs his head yes. "Why don't you call Kat? The shit she says cracks us up!"

"What, you listen to all of my conversations?"

"Yes, but that will end when Dylan goes to prison." He waves as he walks away again.

I decide it would be fun to call Kat from a police station.

"Hey, girl. Guess where I am?"

"Prison?"

I laugh. "Close!"

"Did Ronald McDonald pull you in again?"

"I came to make a complaint against Dylan."

"Why? What happened?"

"He came by the house. I didn't let him in. We yelled at each other through the slider. I called him a fucking liar and a psychopath, and he threatened to kill me."

I cup my hand over the phone and whisper. "He said I was just an easy lay."

Kat chuckles. "Well, that might put a damper on your sex life."

"Yeah, it's not looking too good for me and Dyl."

"Wow, shit, Jen. Are you scared?"

"No, the police are out looking for him now. Did I tell you that he's been stalking and threatening Christine this whole time?"

"No, but I'm not surprised. I'm going to sleep over tonight, okay?"

"Yes, please. Bring Brandy with you."

"Of course! Sorry, I have to go. Joe is yelling for me."

"Okay, see you later."

It feels like it's been forever when the Sergeant swiftly comes back.

"Okay, they have him in the patrol car. I'm going to take you out the side door."

"Seriously?"

"Yes, we want to keep him calm, and I don't want him to see you here."

Sergeant McDonald drops me off at home.

Even though I know they have Dylan, I'm still really nervous. I bolt the front door and wish that I'd put in that security system the builder offered us. I didn't think it was necessary in such a safe town.

# CHAPTER 28

I feel dirty from being in the police station for so long. My legs ache and my body has a chill. I stand under the shower head for twenty minutes before touching the soap. I want to wash away the last five months of my life.

I'm not big on regrets. I don't even regret my two bad marriages. But now, I wish I'd never walked into Barnacle Bill's that night. I wish I'd never met Dylan Jagger. I defended him. I made up excuses for him to my family and friends. And in return, he's humiliated me in the community. I feel such hatred for him. This hate is something I've never felt before. I wish that Dylan had never existed. I can't figure out how he got passed my keen sense of intuition. Is it because I'm so insecure? Will I believe anything coming from a hot guy? How could my instincts be this wrong?

I reassure myself that I didn't know of his issues with anger, and that he never cared that much for me. A week ago, this would have made me sad, but today, I wish him only death. I'm amused by how thin the line is between love and hate. Thank God he never loved me. What he did to Pete's family... how they must miss

Tommy. Christine's life has changed for the worse. She'll always blame herself for Tommy's death. I now know that all that matters to me is that Lauren and Jack are safe.

I wrap myself up in a towel and lie on my bed. I wonder if all the details of our fake relationship will come out in court. Will the prosecutors want to know the intimate details of our sex life? Will they use the fact that he likes to put his hands around my neck and strangle me during sex against him? Prosecuting him won't be easy. He is adorable in every sense of the word. He looks young and innocent. Dylan will try to use his good looks to charm the jurors. That's how he got me to believe his bullshit. He knew I was hooked that night at Barnacle's. I just fell right into his trap. Ugh! What a fucking idiot I am. I can't let him get away with this.

I get myself dressed, dragging my feet. My shame is weighing heavily on me.
I know Kat will be here soon. She'll make me laugh at myself. She'll say, "Welcome to my pathetic world."

I hear scratches at the front door, and look out to see if Kat's car is in the driveway.

I open the door to a smiling dog. "Hi, Brandy, I'm happy to see you."

Kat, speaking for Brandy, says, "Dude, I heard you've been shacking up with a serial killer!"

"Shit, Kat, do you think he is?"

"I think he has to have killed three or more in a certain amount of time. Have you checked under your floor boards?" Kat looks at me and sings the chorus to a Justin Moore song. "You look like I need a drink right now!"

We laugh loudly. Brandy jumps.

"Girl, ain't that the truth! Do you believe all this shit?"

"No, Jen, I can't!"

"Should we sit out on the front porch?"

Kat exclaims, "Why the hell not? You did the right thing, finally!"

"Is that necessary?" I pout.

"I knew it wasn't a good idea to go out with him."

I ask, "What did you know? You knew as much as I did. How could we see through his glossy exterior?"

Kat agrees. "Yes, I have to admit, he's really fucking cute."

"What's that saying? Never judge a book by its cover?"

Kat stops mid-slug. "Especially when he is way prettier than you are."

"Ouch, that hurt!"

Kat makes a sad face. "I'm only kidding, girl. I would do ya!"

"Ew! Shut up, Kat!"

"Oh, Jen, you know you want me."

Wanting to change the subject, I ask her if she wants another drink. No beer tonight—there's no better night to drink hard liquor. We both love to drink raspberry vodka and club soda. She's sweet-talking Brandy when I return with our drinks. I need to talk about something else other than Dylan.

"What's the next big holiday for the farm?"

"Halloween! Joe planted the seeds in July for the corn maze.

Once the stalks get to two feet, he'll cut out the trails."

"I love the maze, but I get lost in it every year. You need to help me get through it this year."

"Let's get through this mess first, Jen."

So much for changing the subject.

# CHAPTER 29

I'm in hibernation mode. I get through most of the weekend without much noise. It's Sunday, and I know I need to update my mom on the horrible predicament I'm in.

John texted me last night that it was okay for the kids to come back to my house. I miss them being here. Things they do that once annoyed me, I now look forward to. The way Jack blows his nose like a fog horn, it's no wonder he gets ear infections all the time. Then there's the loud music Lauren plays all day long, even when she studies. I plan to give them great big hugs when I see them.

After I get my green tea, I climb into the queen's chair and call my mother.

"Jen, I've been chomping at the bit waiting to hear from you!"

"Sorry, Mom, I've been busy being Nancy Drew."

Mom sounds less serious as she says, "Okay, Nancy, what did you find out?"

I can't stop the tears from flowing, "Mom, I found out that

Dylan meant to kill the little boy, Tommy."

"Oh, honey, I'm so sorry!"

"Yeah, he never really cared for me. It was all an act. I feel humiliated. I wish I'd never met him!"

"Honey, are you sure he did it on purpose?"

Remembering that I had left out the infamous pocket-dial from Dylan, I explain, "Well, I left out a big part of the story last week. "It's going to sound bizarre to you, but Dylan pocket-dialed me while he was manhandling Tommy. I wish I'd hung up, but I didn't, and I heard everything. Mom, it was horrible!"

"Okay, you're telling me that you overheard Dylan kill Tommy Butler?"

Exhausted, I say. "Yes!"

Sounding angry, my mom asks, "Why didn't you tell me this before?"

I sniff. "Because I didn't want to believe it."

"Well, what has changed?"

I tell her the whole story. The rest of what I overheard that day between Dylan and Tommy Butler, on the phone. Pete Butler's reaction when he saw his son's lifeless body. The police asking me for help, then bugging my cell phone. Finding out about Dylan's obsession with Christine, Tommy's babysitter, after seeing a picture of them together on Facebook.

"Wait." Mom asks, "What does Tommy's babysitter have to do with it?"

"Well, at first I suspected that Pete Butler had something to do with the murder."

"His own kid, Jen? Why?"

"You're not going to like this, but Dylan killed his mom, he says by accident. Pete helped him cover it up. I thought maybe Pete blackmailed Dylan into killing Tommy."

"Why would he want to kill his own son?"

"I thought it was about the money. He pays child support to Tommy's mom, along with two other women. But when I heard Pete was devastated over losing Tommy, I thought maybe he wasn't involved. Then I found the picture of Dylan with his arm around Christine's waist, and I wondered if they'd been in an illicit relationship. Lauren got me Christine's phone number, and without much convincing, Christine confirmed the relationship between her and Dylan. She told me details of Dylan's abuse towards her. He started stalking her after she ended things with him. He threatened to kill her loved ones if she didn't take him back. Now she blames herself."

I can hear my mom take a deep breath. "This is what's been going on all week? You must be sick over this. Dylan stayed in your house. He was alone with your kids. Did you ever see this side of him?"

"No, Mom, he was a doll to me and the kids. I'm trying not to care about him, but I never knew any of this. Even after he threatened me yesterday."

Mom yells, "What? Did he hurt you?"

"No, Mom, I'm fine. The kids were at John's. We're all good, and Dylan's in jail right now."

"For how long?" she asks, sounding frustrated.

"I don't know how it all works. I hope they don't let him out while waiting for his trial."

"Jen, will you have to go to court to talk about what you heard Dylan do?"

"Yes, because I also heard Dylan tell Tommy to die. That's proof that he knew he was killing him."

"Jesus, Jen, you've gotten yourself into some pickle!"

Agreeing, I say, "I also feel ashamed and embarrassed that I believed that Dylan truly liked me. Here I was, swooning over Dylan while he obsessed over a young beauty. I feel like a stupid old woman!"

Never short of words, she says, "I don't blame you. I feel horrible for you. Maybe you should give dating a break for a while."

"Yes, Mother. I plan to stay hidden from the world as long as possible."

"Jen, I didn't say that, but you *have* made some poor choices in men."

She's pressed me too far. "You think? Mom, I'm aware of my poor taste in men. I gotta go."

"Okay, honey. Be careful. We love you."

I wasn't lying. I really had to go. Lauren had texted me twenty minutes ago to say that her dad was driving them over after his shower. They would be here any minute. I run up to wash my face and brush my teeth, then brush my hair out and put it in a ponytail. I also need to put on a bra. It's weird to be hanging loose when John comes over. This thought makes me laugh out loud. I think most people find my relationship with John odd. Not many divorced couples get along like we do. I tell anyone who questions me how we do it, "We are friends, and both love our kids. No big secret."

I see John's car pull up out front from my bedroom window. I push the window open and yell, "Hi, guys!"

I can see Lauren roll her eyes and John shake his head. I think it's funny that they're not used to me by now. I constantly remind them that they can't love me and hate me for the same reasons.

John steps inside and says, "Hello," while nodding his head.

I grab hold of Jack first and hug him. He nudges me off. "Okay, Mom!" He hates when I touch him. This is the same kid that from infancy to about five years of age wouldn't get off my hip. I couldn't put him down, or he would scream and cry. Not anymore!

Lauren has her arms open, knowing that she's next. I hug her until she lets go.

John hands me a bag that looks like Lauren's and says, "We need to talk."

"Okay, kids, go settle into your rooms. Dad wants to talk to me." I smile at John.

He shakes his head while he walks to the kitchen table. Oh, boy. He has another PowerPoint for me. I sit down next to where he is standing.

"Whatcha got for me?"

He looks up at me and bites his lip. "Well, because of what you finally told the police, that you heard Dylan telling Tommy to die, they have now upped the charge from manslaughter to first-degree murder."

He places a page in front of me. The top of the page says "The Elements of First Degree Murder" in bold print. "Not that this matters in this case, but Dylan's crime is categorized as first-degree murder because he killed a child by use of unreasonable force."

He points at the first bullet point, "intent." He steps back and says, "Dylan intended to kill Tommy."

He points to the second bullet point, "premeditation." He steps back again. "He acted with deliberation and premeditation to kill Tommy. He was aware that Christine, his babysitter, was away, and that Tommy would be home alone while Pete Butler was at work."

The third word is "malice." "Dylan acted with purpose, and with indifference to human life. He wanted to kill Tommy for revenge."

"Okay," I say.

"Jen, since you'll be called as a witness for the prosecution, I want you to know some of the legal terminology."

I feel uneasy. "Okay, thanks."

"The other news is that he was released after the additional questioning. He agreed to the condition that he live at his uncle's home in Woodbridge until his trial. He also agreed to having no contact with you or Christine."

I'm shocked. "But what about how he's been stalking and threatening Christine?"

"She never reported any of the abuse to the police. There's no record of it. It's her word against his. And since he has no priors…"

I cut him off. "What about his mother? He killed his mother!"

"Again, that's a closed case, and inadmissible."

"Oh, my God! Dylan is out there right now?"

"Yes. Oh, I forgot to tell you, the police put an ankle monitor on him. He can't be more than fifty feet from his uncle's house. If he does leave, the police will know it."

"I guess if you feel like it's safe enough for the kids to come back here, then I'm okay with that."

# CHAPTER 30

I make dinner for the kids and myself: ground turkey burger with tomato sauce over linguini. Their favorite. I'm singing along to some old John Denver on the radio when I hear a *bing*. I look at my phone and don't recognize the number. There's a 973 area code. It can't be him. He was told not to contact me or Christine. I open the text.

*I'm sorry I lost my temper. I love you, Jennifer. Please believe me. This is all a misunderstanding.*

I take a big breath. He loves me? I know that it's in my best interest not to take the bait, but I can't resist. There's still this tiny bit of hope that we're all wrong about Dylan. How can he be this bad?

I text back, *who is this?*

A text comes back: *can't say but you know who this is.*

I text back, *you were told not to contact me.*

He ignores my last text and writes, *please believe me. I didn't mean to do what happened. It's all a horrible mistake.*

I find it amusing that he remembers only what he wants to remember. I ask him again what he wants from me.

*Please don't send me up the river.*

He's being very clever in not giving himself away. If I bring these texts to the police, they'll say that there's no proof that they're from Dylan. God knows where he got this phone. He can charm anyone to do anything for him. But then, something tells me that this isn't Dylan.

*Listen, mystery person, I will not back down. I will tell them what I heard. I don't want you to able to do this again. And you need to pay for what you did.*

In all caps, they text back, *THEN YOU WILL PAY!*

Wait. These texts sound like a prank. I look back at the first text, and it says "Jennifer." Dylan never called me by my full name. Maybe it's one of Jack's friends. That's something they might do. I write nothing back.

I bang the wall to tell the kids that dinner is ready. They come pounding down the steps. We sit down to eat. Trying to avoid the subject of Dylan, I ask what they've been up to.

Lauren answers, "I've been studying for my SAT subject test on Biology."

"Good for you, Lauren. I'm sure you'll ace it. How about you, Jack?"

"I'm trying to read the five books required for Junior English."

I try to pretend to be interested in the topic of Junior English, but all I can think about are the texts I had received earlier. I give up on my plan to avoid talking about Dylan. "Hey Jack, don't get mad…but is there any way your friends would text me pretending to be Dylan?"

He laughs and says, "Hate to say it, but yeah, they would. The guys have been giving me a lot of shit about you and Dylan."

"I'm sorry, Jack. Bad shit?"

"Nah. Don't worry, Mom. Nothing I can't handle."

They are both gorging themselves with pasta. I think they want to eat and run away from me and my problems.

"Not to bring up Dylan again, but did Dad tell you that he's up north at his uncle's house with an ankle monitor keeping track of his whereabouts?"

Jack says with confidence, "Mom, I'm not scared of him. I've got, like, fifty pounds on him! He's not going to do anything to us."

Lauren nods her head, agreeing with Jack with a mouthful of pasta.

I nod. "Okay, then we're all good?"

They both nod yes.

After dinner, while I'm cleaning the dishes, I can't help checking out the window. I'm not as sure as Jack is. The police think that an ankle monitor is going to stop him. If he wants to get to me, he will. A chill runs down my spine. He can't blame me for his arrest. He was the last person to see Tommy alive. I'm just confirming that he did it. Ugh! I need a Kat fix.

I ring her on her cell. No answer. Oh God, she's avoiding me too. But a second later, she calls me back.

"Hey, Jen. How're you doing?"

"No cracks about dating a serial killer?"

"No, I'm too tired today. Long weekend at work."

"Is your back bothering you?"

"Killing me!" Kat exclaims.

I brag, "This week is my last one off before I start back with Kev."

"Damn, girl, I wish I had your life! Wait, scratch that. Your life is too fucked up with people dying and shit!"

"There's the girl I know and love!"

I can imagine her pulling at her shirt. "Yeah, I'm in here somewhere under all this dirt! What's the latest?"

"Let's see; the police have upped his charge to first-degree murder, he has to live with his uncle, and he has an ankle monitor."

"Shit, Jen, the police think that's going to keep him away from here?"

"I guess."

"Well, if I were you, I'd get some more deadbolts put on my doors."

Laughing, I say, "I plan to."

"Hey Jen, I know I joke around a lot, but this is serious shit here. This dude has, for real, killed two people, that we know of. Please promise me that you're not gonna get all "momma hen" and try to save him."

"Kat, I promise. It was all fun and games with him, but now I feel stupid that I ever even dated him in the first place. I'm over him!"

"Hang in there, girl. I need to go water the plants in the greenhouse before I go. Talk later?"

"Yup, bye."

It's not often that Kat turns off her funny switch to be serious, but when she does, I like her even more.

# CHAPTER 31

It's early Monday morning, and I'm already dreading the day ahead. I plan to call Dr. Thorne after my morning run with Riley.

I drink a few glasses of cold water and we hit the pavement. It's a little after 6 a.m., with not many cars on the road. My favorite time of the day, these days. I start to run, imagining that the world is all mine and no one else lives in it. No one to judge me or place blame on me. When I was a teenager, I wanted to be famous. The idea of being adored by so many fascinated me. To be rich, to have big homes and lots of cars, and to buy whatever fit my fancy. But now, I want to hide away and live a quiet, private life. It would be nice to be widely known for something heroic, like saving someone from a sinking car. But even then, they would find out about my failed marriages and call me a two-time loser. You can't win these days, especially now. I'm screwed. This relationship with Dylan will follow me forever. A relationship with a killer will make me famous for all the wrong reasons.

I try to appreciate the gorgeous morning. Riley is full of energy. I start to perk up. I'm running at a faster pace than usual. I can get through this mess. I have family and friends that still love and support me. I don't want to admit this to myself, but I do miss him. I miss Dylan. I miss waking up to his smile. I miss playing with his bedhead in the morning. I've been on both sides of breakups, but this one has been involuntary. Dylan's crime gives me no choice. To stop seeing him is one thing, but to stop loving him is another. I need Dr. Thorne in this department. She'll help me find some solace.

After I get home, I call Dr. Thorne's office, and she picks up the line.

"Jen, are you ok?"

"I guess you've heard, then?"

"Yes. I have a 10 a.m. opening. Can you make it?"

"I'll be there."

After cooling down, I eat some Cheerios. I can't help checking on my kids. I crack their doors and peek in. Each is sleeping soundly, thank God. Now I'm in need of another long, warm shower. I can't wait to see the water bills after all this is over.

I pull up to Dr. Thorne's office early. I'm always early to everything. I remember that the morning of my wedding to John, my limousine was an hour late to pick me up to go to the church. John said that he felt panicked because I was never late. I kind of liked that he was worried. Kat would say, "Keep them guessing, girl!"

It looks like Dr. Thorne's last patient is walking out of her office building. I suddenly have an overwhelming need to cry.

Wiping my tears away, I say, "Hi, Dr. Thorne. Thanks again for seeing me today."

"Oh, honey, it looks like you need some attention."

"Yes, I'm a bit of a disaster."

"Sit down. Tell me what's going on."

"Well, I'm having a hard time compartmentalizing my feelings about Dylan. On one hand, I hate him for what he has done, but on the other hand, I miss him. I think I might even still love him. I feel bad about that. I'm glad that Tommy will get justice, but I hate that I'm the prosecutor's main witness, who will help put him away forever."

"Jen, this is a lot to process. Give yourself time to mourn this loss. It may take you a bit longer to heal because of his upcoming trial. You start up work again next week, right?"

"Thankfully, yes. I'm looking forward to playing all day with my little man, Kev."

"Jen, I want to counsel you the way I would any patient after a break-up. But your situation is more complicated, even for me. I know how much you felt for this man. You took such wonderful care of him after his surgery. The feelings you have for Dylan are based on his deceit. He has you thinking that he's the perfect man for you. He makes sure that you can't see who he really is. He controls you by lying about how he really feels. He's a mirage."

Frowning, I say, "The problem is, it took me too long to see the real Dylan. He was able to kill Tommy."

"Oh, Jen, you can't blame yourself for any of that. You're doing all you can for Tommy now. Mourning is a process. I ask patients to acknowledge and accept the feelings that come along with a loss: depression, anger, and hopelessness. For you, I need to add the feelings of guilt, revenge, embarrassment, and victimhood."

Dr. Thorne leans in and places her hand on mine. "Jennifer, I promise to help you get through this. We can work out all these feelings together."

Fifteen minutes into our session, my sadness has lifted. Dr. Thorne helps me see that all is not lost. That in time I will heal, but that it might take longer for me because of the trial.

"Dr. Thorne, you don't think I'm crazy for still caring about him, do you?"

"No, Jen, you're mourning the loss of this 'perfect man.' He convinced you that he was kind, sweet, and loving. He's not any of those things. If you can accept that the relationship was just fantasy, then you can start to move forward. I'm advising against starting any new relationships until you can wake up in the morning and not think of Dylan."

I throw my hands in the air. "Don't worry, doc. I'm sworn off men forever!"

# CHAPTER 32

For three straight days, it has been nice and calm in my home. Jack and Lauren are preparing to go back to school, so they hardly leave their rooms. I text them to see what they want for lunch, and bring it up to them. I insist that they come down for dinner so that we can be together in one room for a few minutes. I'm keeping dinners simple: hamburgers, baked chicken, and pizza. Anything I can find in the freezer.

I haven't left my property, not even for a run. Dr. Thorne said it would be a good idea for me to take up a new hobby. I had a plan to pick up crocheting right before I met Dylan, and I have all the tools to start a project, so I watch a few YouTube videos on how to crochet. I have to watch it ten times before I get the hang of it. The first few hats I make are lopsided, but my last one is perfect. I even wear it inside the house. When Lauren sees me, she keeps asking me to take it off, which makes me want to wear it more. Keeping busy is good for me. I have a list of projects that I need to get done before the end of summer. With only a few days left, I get to it. One job is cleaning out the kitchen cabinets. Not only do I clean them, I put down a shelf liner in each. The fridge is now clean, too.

It feels good to get back to my dull, everyday life. I'm enjoying binge-watching shows like *Cheers* and *The X-Files*. It's amazing how many hours they can take out of one's day. I feel like I'm starting to heal. Even though I'm thankful that I haven't heard from Dylan, it does sting a bit. I keep telling myself what Dr. Thorne said, that he was a mirage. I'm only allowing positive thoughts into my head.

I'm going to bed early and eating well, things that one would do if they were physically sick. My illness just happens to be mental. The air conditioner temperature is set to 67 degrees. I need to use lots of blankets to keep me warm at night now. I'm not drinking any alcohol for now either, at Dr. Thorne's request. She said that sobriety clears the cobwebs out of one's brain.

After dinner, I start my ritual of taking a long, hot shower, then get into my nightclothes and lay in bed with all the covers pulled up to my chin. I watch a bit of television, then turn the lights off at 9 p.m. Tonight is no exception. I fall asleep thinking about which fun park I'll take Kevin to on my first day back babysitting.

I awake suddenly. Something isn't right. I try to open my eyes. Black. All I see is black. I can't catch my breath. I try to sit up, but my arms are pinned. There's something heavy on my chest. I panic. Someone is holding me down. I try to fight, but can't move. Crying, I realize I'm being smothered. Is this Dylan? He's suffocating me. Why?

I try to roll, and manage to kick my legs free. I kick and bang them down on the bed. *Someone, please, hear me!* My hands are grabbing at the sheets. I dig my fingers into to the bed, trying to move away from him. There's a sharp pain in my shoulders—he's kneeling on me. I scream, but hear nothing. I can't get any air. There's a loud bang that sounds like it might have been the lamp. I can't breathe. I can't breathe.

I'm starting to fade. I can't get any air. I'm crying, but there's no sound; pleading for help, but no one can hear me. I think of Lauren and Jack. *I'm so sorry! I'm so sorry!*

*Thump!*

The weight is gone. Breathing in, I push the pillow up from my face. Everything is blurry. Searching the room, I see that the bedroom door is open. Light is streaming from the hallway, and there's a figure standing at the end of my bed.

It's Lauren. She's panting, leaning over, and holding something big in her hands

In between breaths, she gets out, "Mom, are you okay? Mom, are you okay?"

I try to focus. "Yes, what happened?"

Out of breath, she points. "It's Dylan, Mom. It's Dylan."

I look down to the floor and see Dylan lying on his side in a fetal position. He isn't moving, and appears unconscious. His chest is still rising.

She swings her Biology book in the air like a baseball bat. "I knocked him off you like this." Lauren starts to cry. "Mom, he was killing you! He almost killed you!"

Adrenaline rushing through me, heart racing, I drop my legs

off the side of the bed. I look at Dylan. He's still, but his chest is rising. He's still alive. I watch him. Suddenly, his eyes open. Fear and panic takes over my body. I pick up my pillow with both hands and pounce onto Dylan, holding the pillow on his face. I lean forward and drop my body weight down onto it.

Lauren cries out, "Mom, stop! What are you doing?"

I apply more pressure. I still can't breathe. "I will *not* let him hurt us!"

Dylan stays still. The room is silent. It must be over. I sit back and get back onto the edge of my bed, still holding the pillow.

"Lauren, we're safe now. Please call Sergeant McDonald."

Her eyes widen with panic. "I don't know his number."

I wipe the hair from my face. "Get my phone. He's in the contacts."

Lauren grabs my phone and presses his number. "Mom, it's ringing. What do I say?"

I extend my hand. "Here, give me the phone."

She hands me the phone. I can hear Sergeant McDonald asking, "Who is this? Hello?"

Trying to focus, I say, "This is Jennifer Burns. I just killed Dylan Jagger in self-defense. We're in my bedroom. Can you please come over to my house?"

"Shit, Jen, you okay?"

"Yes, please just come."

I hang up, not knowing if he'll call the rest of the police or if he'll come alone.

Jack comes running into my room with his Xbox gaming

headset around his neck.

"Mom, what the hell happened? Is that Dylan? Is he dead?"

I sit on the edge of my bed, looking down at Dylan's lifeless body. "Yes, and yes. The police are on their way."

Jack rushes onto the bed next to me, putting his arm around my shoulders. Pulling me closer to comfort me, he says, "I didn't hear anything, Mom. I'm sorry I wasn't here to help you, but it looks you did okay on your own." He gives me a little smile.

I look over at him and smirk. "Lauren hit him with her Biology book. Whacked him right off me. He was trying to smother me."

Jack looks over at Lauren, who's hugging a pillow from my bed. "Way to go, sis!"

I get serious. "Okay, listen, both of you. I was the only one in this room tonight. Lauren, you were never here. Do you hear me?"

Lauren asks, "But what about me hitting him with my book?"

"We can leave that out. This is a problem I brought into our home. I will be the only one to resolve it."

Hearing those words coming out of my mouth brings tears to Lauren's eyes. She says, "Okay, I was never here. Thanks, Mom."

"No, thank *you*. Now pick up your book and go put it in your room. I'll do all of the talking with the police. Lauren, you were studying with music playing, and Jack, you had headphones on. Neither of you knew anything until after it was over and I came to get you. We clear?"

In unison, Lauren and Jack say, "Clear!"

We all turn our heads when we hear someone knocking at the

front door.

"Jack, please go let Sergeant McDonald in."

Jack runs down the stairs. I can't stop staring at Dylan, lying there on the floor. I feel bad that it has comes to this. But he came into my home, where my kids are, and tried to end my life. He tried to eternally silence me. Well, we stopped him. I mean, *I* stopped him. What's my story? I have only seconds to prepare.

Jack yells, "Mom, we're coming up."

I don't move. I can't move. My body is too heavy. I think I might be in shock. I wonder if he will read me my rights before asking me any questions. Will he place me under arrest?

Jack walks in with two men behind him. Who could that second man be? Did Sergeant McDonald call John? I see the Sergeant, and then the other man pushes him aside and runs to Dylan's body. Oh, my God, it's Pete Butler. The Sergeant has brought Pete Butler.

The Sergeant walks over to Dylan's body and leans down to feel his neck. Seeing him do this makes something explodes inside me, and I begin to wail. Jack and the Sergeant grab both sides of me. Pete stays still, staring down at the body. I can't stop crying. I'm shaking like crazy. Lauren grabs the blanket from my bed and wraps it around me.

I start to rock back and forth. "I didn't mean to. He was trying to smother me. The kids were in the house. I got an arm free and pushed him off me. He fell to the floor. There was a loud bang. I don't think he was moving, but I knew I had to stop him from trying again. I grabbed my pillow and put it over his face and sat on him. I held tight. I couldn't let him kill me and then the kids."

The Sergeant comes over to me and whispers in my ear, "Please ask the kids to go their rooms."

His voice is loud enough for the kids to hear. They both get up and start to move towards the door.

Lauren leans over to ask, "Mom, are you okay?"

I nod my head yes.

The kids quietly leave the room and close the door behind them.

I'm sobbing uncontrollably, gasping for air. My eyes and nose are running all down my nightshirt. I'm scared and embarrassed. I grab the blanket tight around me. The Sergeant gets up and whispers something in Pete's ear. Pete bobs his head yes, then kneels next to Dylan and leans over him. I can't see what he's doing. Moments later, he sits back on his feet. He puts both hands over his face and begins to rock. He's crying, but it's unclear to me whether Pete is happy or sad.

The Sergeant kneels in front of me. He grabs both my hands and says, "Listen to me, this wasn't your fault. Do you hear me? This wasn't your fault."

I glance into his eyes, which are welling up. I nod my head yes.

"Pete and I will take care of this. You'll be cleared of any wrongdoing. He got what was coming to him. He was bigger and stronger than you. You fought him off, and he hit his head. He threatened to kill you and your kids. You got control and held the pillow over his face. You used all your body weight. You fought back. You had to protect your family. Jen." He shakes my shoulders to make me look at him. "Jen, does this sound about right?"

"Yes." I answer.

Pete stands up and comes over to me. He sits down on the bed next to me and puts his arms around me, pulling me tightly against his body so hard that I lose my breath. He kisses my cheek not once, but several times, and says, "Thank you, Jen! Thank you for getting Tommy justice! You have done a great thing for my family. Jen, he had us all fooled. He was pure evil!"

Sergeant McDonald moves towards the door. "Okay, Pete, you have to go now. I'm going to call this in."

Pete gives me one more bear hug. He kisses my head as he gets up to leave.

"Jen, you have saved my life!"

I wonder what he means, but I'm focusing on what the Sergeant is saying on the phone to the police.

"I have a ten-one-hundred inside the house of Jennifer Burns. Please send an ambulance to 23 Poplar Lane."

The voice responds, "Ten-four."

Shaking my head back and forth, I try to get up from the edge of the bed. "No, I don't want to go to the hospital!"

Sergeant McDonald slowly presses his hands down on my shoulders and says, "Jen, please sit down. You're in shock. We need to get you checked out. This has been a very traumatic event for you. Please trust me, okay?"

I feel like a child. I think about what he just said. Am I hurt? Do I need medical attention? I do trust him. I oblige.

# CHAPTER 33

In the ambulance, the attendants are talking above me, like I'm not here. I wonder if I'm awake. They're saying things like "blood pressure—too high" and "pulse—way too fast." One attendant says that my heart is going to explode. I try to speak to them, but I can't stop shaking. Is it from fear, or am I just cold?

I hear one attendant say, "Here, put this blanket on her and raise her legs up."

Relief.

I feel something being put on my face, and I push it away as hard as I can. "What is that? What are you doing to me? Stop!"

Someone is holding my hand. Someone else is rubbing my arm. I see only men.

I hear someone say, "Get that oxygen on her, and start an IV."

Now the person holding my hand is holding my arm down. *Oh, my God! Get off me!* I try to fight.

From the front of the ambulance, someone says, "Forty-five, white, female. Showing signs of emotional trauma; disoriented, shaking, and not responding to questions. Skin is pale and shows no signs of cuts or bruising."

I try to sit up, but straps are holding me down. "Calm down," I tell myself. Why would these strangers want to hurt me? *Calm down.*

The vehicle jerks to a stop, and the attendants jump up. The door is open, and I can see red and white lights blinking. I want my kids. Where are my kids? They pull me out of the ambulance. I hear the wheels lock in place, and then they're wheeling me into the building. It's bright yellow inside. I can't keep my eyes open. Tears run down my face. I hear female voices talking. *Okay, now I'm safe. They will protect me.*

I see a women's face, and ask her, "What's happening to me? Where are my kids?"

They move me to a bed in a room with radiant white walls. I hear a familiar voice. It's John, talking to someone. Yeah, John is here. Does he have our kids?

I see John's face. He's talking to me. I hear him say, "You almost died!" I try to concentrate, but cannot understand what else he's saying. His mouth is moving and he looks upset. I'm starting to feel sleepy. John is still standing next to my bed, holding onto my forearm. He hasn't touched me in fifteen years. I killed Dylan. My eyelids are getting heavy. I want to sleep. Sleep.

# CHAPTER 34

I'm awake. The sun's rays peek through the blinds. It's morning. I'm relieved to see Lauren sitting at the end of my bed and Jack's silhouette in front of the window. I hear loud beeping sounds.

John's voice makes me look right. He leans down and asks, "Jen, how do you feel?"

Lauren and Jack jump towards my bed. "Mom!"

I move my hand towards my chest. "I'm okay. My chest hurts and my shoulders feel sore.

I push myself up into a sitting position. "Is Dylan really dead?" I ask.

Lauren comes up to the side of the bed and puts her hand on my arm. She says, "Mom, Dylan broke into our house last night and tried to kill you by putting a pillow over your face."

I shake my head with frustration. "I know that, but is he dead?"

"Yes, he's dead." She is squeezing my arm way too hard. "You put a pillow over his face and he died."

I shake my head in disbelief. "I know I tried to kill him, but-

"

Jack jumps in and yells, "Yes, but he deserved it, Mom. He was going to kill you."

I scratch my head with both hands and look straight at Lauren. "Who told you that he's dead?"

Lauren stretches to hug me. "Sergeant McDonald said he was dead last night."

She places her head on my lap and wraps her arms around my legs. "Mom, it's okay, you were protecting us."

A man in a white coat enters the room. He asks Lauren, Jack, and John to leave the room for a few minutes. He says, "Hello, Jennifer. I'm Dr. Laing. I admitted you to the hospital last night. Dr. Thorne will be in to see you this morning. You've been through a traumatic experience. We were worried about you last night, but your vitals are getting better."

"Doctor, why does my chest hurt?"

"You have two cracked ribs. You'll feel better in a few days."

I nod and say, "Okay."

I can remember trying to breathe and the pressure on my chest. Dylan was on top of me?
The doctor keeps talking, but I'm not hearing what he's saying. He leaves the room. I look for Jack and Lauren, but no one comes. I feel my breath getting heavy. I'm starting to panic. My ribs hurt even more. I drink water from a cup I find on the table next to my bed. I remember last night; seeing only darkness, trying to breathe, being unable to move, and feeling hopeless.

My thoughts are interrupted by a knock at the door. It's Dr. Thorne. I start to tremble, then cry. She walks swiftly toward me. "Jennifer, you're okay. You're going to be fine."

"Dr. Thorne, they're telling me that Dylan is dead."

I can feel her hand through the blanket on my bed. She is patting my calf. "Jennifer, from what John and Dr. Laing have told me, you have suffered a traumatic event. Dylan trying to harm you triggered, inside you, a fight-or-flight reaction. Luckily, you chose to fight and you survived. The adrenaline that poured into your body caused you symptoms similar to a heart attack. When you were admitted, you were trembling and your heart was racing."

I look up at Dr. Thorne and meekly ask, "When can I go home?"

"Today, if Dr. Laing agrees that you're physically stable enough."

"I'm good, Dr. Thorne. I really want to go home!"

"Okay, Jen, I'll see what I can do." Dr. Thorne leaves the room.

Jack and Lauren walk back into my room holding coffees. *When did my kids start drinking coffee?* John is trailing behind them.

Jack says, "Mom, I heard Dr. Thorne tell the other doctor that you want to go home. Is this true?"

"Yes, the doctor says I only have a few cracked ribs. I want to be in my own bed."

A nurse enters the room and takes my vitals. She looks at my IV bag and says nothing. She writes something on her clipboard and leaves the room. Jack and Lauren look at each other and shrug.

Minutes later, Dr. Laing comes back into the room. "Your vitals are all normal. You can leave as soon as you sign some paperwork."

I nod and say, "Thank you, doctor."

"Take care of yourself, Ms. Burns," He says.

Lauren takes a pair of sweats out of a bag she's holding. She tells me that the police took the clothes I was wearing last night. I know why they did that. I killed someone.

The nurse wheels me out to John's car. I get into the front seat. No one says anything on the way home. I can't wait to lie down in my bed.

John parks in the driveway and runs around to help me out of the car. I can't help holding my hand against my ribs. I get up the stairs to my room and find that nothing's different. The bed is even made. Jack pulls open the covers and I climb in. Lauren pulls down the shades. I need to rest. I want to sleep.

Before they leave the room, they ask if I need anything. I ask them to turn down the light, but not to turn it off. I suddenly feel afraid of the dark.

I lie awake for hours with my eyes wide open, staring at the ceiling. Scared of being alone, I listen for sounds of Lauren and Jack in the house.

# CHAPTER 35

I wake thinking that it has only been a few minutes. I look at my phone to see that it is 7 a.m. I smell bacon. John must be here. He's the only one who cooks bacon for breakfast. I can see light coming through under the shade. I slept all night. I sit up. *Ouch, my ribs.* I sit on the side of the bed and stare down at the floor. I try to remember how Dylan looked lying there.

Lauren knocks lightly while she walks in. "Mom, how are you today?"

Seeing her beautiful face expressing concern warms my heart. "No worries, sweetheart, I'll be fine." I look back at the floor.

Lauren comes over to my side and helps me stand up. "Let's get something to eat."

"Now you're taking care of me?"

She smiles. "Yes, Mother, you need a little tender loving care."

"Okay. Is your father here? I smell bacon."

Lauren nods yes, and giggles. "Yup, and he's made you a feast downstairs!"

I walk into the kitchen. "Thanks John, you didn't have to do all this."

"Anything for a hero!"

"I'm no hero," I moan, climbing into a chair.

"Yes, you are. You protected our kids from him."

"From who?"

Jack chimes in. "Mom, seriously, you don't remember what Dylan did to you? He was trying to kill you!"

After breakfast, John goes off to work. Lauren and Jack go back to their rooms, and I'm left alone. I ascend into my comfy bed with my laptop. I want to see what the world is saying about what has happened. I open my Facebook page, and I have fifty-three notifications. Why so many? I press on one of them and then another. I read them all. The people from the Tree Lawn community are reaching out to me in droves. Some are writing that I'm a hero, and that Dylan Jagger had it coming to him. All hope that I feel better. One woman named Sue has started something called a "meal train." Women are signing up to bring me meals. I shudder at the thought. I don't want people coming to my house with food. I can't handle all this praise. Don't they know I ended someone's life? I stop reading and slap my laptop closed.

I try to close my eyes to sleep, but can't get the word "hero" out of my head. This is a mistake. I'm no hero, if I killed another human being. I know it was in self-defense, but that makes this no less horrific. How can they be rejoicing? They say that Tommy got justice. I can't stop replaying what happened in my head. I can't stop thinking *if only I had just left Dylan on the floor and let the police take care of it.* Why did I have to kill him?

I call Lauren on her cell. "Hey, honey, can you come in here?"

"Be right there!"

Lauren opens my door. "Do you need something, Momma?"

"Yes. I want you to help me remember a few things. First, were you in the room when it happened?"

Lauren plops down next to me on the bed. "Ouch!" I grab my ribs.

"Oh, sorry, Mom! Yes, I heard something bang, and when I came in to check on what it was, I saw Dylan on top of you. I hit him off you with my Biology book. He was unconscious on the floor over there." She points to the floor on my side of the bed.

I look and try to see an outline of the body. "He was on his side, right? I remember putting a pillow over his face in that position."

Lauren tilts her head. "Yes, why?"

"Well, I don't think I could have killed him in that position. Even if I sat on him."

Lauren interrupts, "You did sit on him."

"I know, but something tells me that it wouldn't have been enough to kill him."

Lauren ponders this idea. "Mom, I see what you're saying, but Sergeant McDonald said he was dead."

"Lauren, did you or I check to see if he was breathing?"

"No way, I was too scared to go near him again."

"I can't wrap my head around this. You can go back to your

studies. Thanks for your help."

She kisses my cheek and says, "Call me if you need me."

This reminds me that I need to see Dr. Thorne, and soon.

Before I try to sleep, I call John.

"Hi, Jen. You okay?"

"Yes, fine. This morning, with the kids here, I was unable to talk to you. Can you do me a favor?"

John sounds curious. "Yeah, sure, what?"

"Can you get the results of Dylan's autopsy?"

"Yes, I'm sure I can. What are you thinking?"

"I need to know exactly how he died." My voice is shaky. "Please, I need to know what it says."

"Okay, okay. As soon as I hear anything I will call you. Jen, please remind yourself that you saved yourself and our kids by doing what you did. Stop looking for answers right now and get some rest."

"Okay." Taking his advice, I turn off my phone. I lie back and close my eyes.

# CHAPTER 36

It feels like hours later when I wake up. I turn my cell back on, and it starts to beep. I look down to see several texts and missed calls. I look at Kat's texts first. The most recent says, *fuck it, I'm just coming over.*

I need to take a shower. I cautiously get up. My ribs pang. The shower feels nurturing. I try to wash away the fact that I might have really killed Dylan. My intuition tells me that I didn't. An internal battle is going on in my head. My family, who I trust, is telling me that I caused Dylan's death, but my gut tells me that I didn't. Am I in denial? Is my mind protecting me? Dr. Thorne said to give it some time. I put my head forward and let the water just roll off. I look down at my feet and see bruises on my ribs and arms, making this all too real.

While toweling off, I hear sounds of a ruckus outside the door. It must be Kat, demanding to see me. I walk out of the bathroom right into her.

"What the fuck, Jen? What happened here last night?"

I wrap the towel tighter around my boobs. "Kat, please ease

up. This is nothing to joke about."

Kat steps back and frowns. "Sorry girl, you know I love ya."

Looking down at my wet feet, I say, "That's good, Kat, because I'm going to need your support more than ever now."

I adjust my towel so I can sit on the side of my bed. "Somehow Dylan got into this house last night without us knowing. He tried to kill me by shoving a pillow on my face and using his knees to hold me down."

Kat puts her hand to her mouth. "Dylan broke into your house with the sole purpose to kill you?"

I nod yes.

"I'm so sorry, Jen. How the hell did you get him off you?"

I put my finger to my lips, lean over to her, and whisper, "Lauren clubbed him in the head with her Biology book and he fell to the floor. But the part about Lauren is secret. I'm leaving her out of this fucking mess."

"Okay, so you pushed him off." She winks.

What's weird is that he didn't even try to fight me off him. He didn't move. Dr. Thorne says I had to fight. I thought I had to kill him."

"Jesus, Jen, remind me never to piss you off!"

I look at Kat. "Really?"

She puts both hands up. "Alright, sorry. Dylan's really dead?"

I look down at the floor. "Yes. That part is true."

"Oh, my God, Jen! I'm so sorry. What can I do to help?"

"Just stay and make me laugh."

She jumps up on the bed, smiling, and says, "You got it!"

I go back into the bathroom to get dressed. Getting on clothes takes a bit of time. My ribs hurt with every twist and turn.

"Everything okay in there?" Kat yells to me.

I come out of the bathroom dressed and ready. "Kat, there is something strange here."

Kat smirks. "Stranger than Dylan trying to kill you?"

I twinge. "Yes, my gut is telling me that something is not right."

She scratches the side of her tangled pony tail. "Well, I definitely trust your gut more than mine."

I lean over to comb out my wet hair. "No, I was all messed up from almost dying myself. I remember seeing Sergeant McDonald check Dylan's wrist. Did I tell you that he brought Pete with him?"

"What? Tommy's dad? Why the hell did he bring him?"

"I don't know. They both came into my room and took over. I remember the Sergeant kneeling in front of me, explaining to me what had just happened. It was like he was telling me a story about someone else."

Kat is shaking her head. "Maybe he was making sure you didn't get arrested for murder!" She puts one hand up. "Not that this was murder. But maybe he wants it to be an open-and-shut case of self-defense."

I nod to Kat. "That's probably it. I need to just accept what has happened and stop overthinking it. I'll focus on my ribs healing and getting back to the life I had before Dylan. Do you know that people in this town are calling me a hero? They want to bring me dinners."

Kat makes a gross face.

"Yeah, right? I hate all this attention! Especially for something this bad. And believe me, soon enough they will make me into a villain. John's going to get Dylan's autopsy results for me."

Kat pinches her nose. "Are you sad about Dylan being gone?"

Nodding, I say, "Yes and no. I'm sad that I'll never see Dylan smile again and he drove me to murder. But I'm glad that this is over. I'm happy for Pete and his family. It's hard to know what to miss about Dylan. Dr. Thorne says he was just a mirage. My brain is trying to believe that I'm the one responsible for ending someone's life. I know that I'll wake up tomorrow and be ridden with anxiety and guilt, but right now I'm just happy to be sitting here with you. I would have missed my Kat."

"Aw," Kat bends in to give me a hug.

Needing to talk about anything else, I ask, "What's going on with the Bachelor?"

We both chuckle.

# CHAPTER 37

The next day, I try to get back to all the emails and texts from family and friends. I just say, "thank you," and don't answer the questions asking for more details. I don't want to rehash what happened over and over again. There are no negative comments yet. They're all positive and congratulatory. I can't wait for this fifteen minutes of fame to be over.

Sergeant McDonald called me earlier, and as we predicted, there will be no charges brought against me for the death of Dylan Jagger. He used my full name, Jennifer Burns, when he asked for me. His tone sounded official. He must have been calling from the station. Oh yes, and my cell phone still has a bug in it. It's a relief to know that this nightmare is over. Dylan's crimes are now closed cases. There's no one to prosecute.

Deciding that it's time for some real help, I call Dr. Thorne. After the sixth ring, an answering machine picks up. "Hey, Dr. Thorne. It's me, Jen Burns. I need to make an appointment to see you. Maybe some time—"

She picks up the line. "Jennifer! Hi, how are you?"

I answer, "I'm hanging in there. Do you have any time

available today?"

"Yes, how is three o'clock?"

"I'll be there."

The hours in the day are filled with people stopping by with food and all the niceties that come with it. I feel foolish accepting the food and all the accolades. I feel like what I did is terrible. My kids keep reminding me that I could have died. I saved myself along with them. I try to take all the praise in stride. I write to Sue on Facebook messenger to tell her how much I appreciate this meal train that she was kind enough to start, but try to emphasize how unnecessary it is. That I'm fine, and will be making a trip out to the grocery store very soon.

There hasn't been a response yet.

I text John, *Any news on the autopsy?*

He texts me back, *Yes, but I want to talk to you in person.*

Oh, shit! *What?*

*I will stop by on my way home from work.*

*Fine!*

I've been holding off on calling my mother until I hear about the autopsy results. She'll be even more worried about me if I tell her I killed someone. I know that she'll ask me too many questions. She doesn't even know that Dylan is dead yet. I told the kids not to tell her.

Deciding that sleep is the best medicine for me right now, I crawl back under the sheets. Losing my anonymity is exhausting. I want the boring life I had before Dylan came along.

I feel someone nudging me. I grab their hand and squeeze.

"Easy, Mom. It's just me, Lauren."

I feel embarrassed that I scared her.

"You said to wake you up by 2:30 p.m. for your appointment with Dr. Thorne."

"Thanks, honey. Okay, I'll get up." I'm looking forward to talking to Dr. Thorne.

Driving is a bit scary. My nerves are still on edge. I feel like I don't have total control of the car. I make it to her office building and park in the street.

Dr. Thorne opens the door and finds me cross-legged in her waiting room.

She extends her hand, saying, "Happy to see you. You look better than you did a few days ago, Jen. You were really pale in the hospital."

I follow her in and sit on the designated patient's couch. I'm looking around, much more aware of my surroundings. "Dr. Thorne, I feel like all my senses are heightened. I'm too nervous and jumpy. Is all this normal?"

"Oh, Jennifer, anything new that you might be feeling or experiencing is all normal. You've been through a traumatic event. You were attacked and had to defend yourself by ending another person's life. Both come with an aftermath of anxiety and depression. There's no quick fix here. You need to give yourself many months to heal."

"I know that I do, but I just want to be the old fun Jen again. I miss her. I'm having a hard time feeling happiness. People are saying that I'm a hero, but I disagree with them."

Dr. Thorne hands me a small leather-bound notebook. "Jen, I want you to write down anything you want in this notebook. It can be anything from the weather to why you hate the mailman."

I smile. "I don't hate the mailman!"

She smiles back at me. "You know what I mean?"

I nod yes.

She explains, "I'm not sure how to gauge how you're doing without these details. Write down times of the day when you feel good or bad. If someone upsets you, write down what upset you and why. Nothing is off-limits."

I tuck the brown book down next to me on the couch. I face her and say, "I'm concerned about my lack of guilt. Does this make me less human?"

Dr. Thorne says, "Maybe we can put that emotion aside for now. You have enough on your plate right now with being attacked by someone you cared for."

"But doc, part of me thinks that it's my intuition telling me not to feel guilty."

Dr. Thorne frowns. "The mind can play many tricks on us, Jen. This is a very heavy thing you need to handle. Try to focus on what you're feeling, rather than what you're not?"

"Okay, I'll try."

# CHAPTER 38

I can't wait to get home. John will be here in an hour, and so will the news that I've been waiting for. This information will determine my guilt or innocence. I know that it will make no difference in the case, but I just need to know what exactly killed him.

John arrives later than I anticipated. When I'm anxious, I tend to talk too loud.

As soon as I start to ask John questions, he raises his hand to tell me to calm down. We sit on the front porch. It feels weird, just the two of us. I ask what the results were.

Slowly, he says, "He died of asphyxiation."

Seeing me lower my head in defeat, he reacts. "But he also had a broken neck."

I put my hand over my mouth. "Oh my God. Lauren! She can never know this!"

He nods. "I figured you would say that. This would kill her. Hell, she wants to study to be a doctor!"

"What are the police saying about these results?"

"Sergeant said to me that these results were for our eyes only.

He said that the case is closed."

"Oh, thank God! Okay, I'll accept that I killed Dylan now. We all need to move on and put this far behind us."

He smiles and stands. "Sounds like a plan. See ya later." He waves as he walks down the porch stairs.

I stay seated. The weight of this information is paralyzing. Now I know that I have to accept that I killed Dylan. Me alone. I make a promise to myself that Lauren will never know the autopsy results. I will smile when people commend me, and grin and bear it when they vilify me. This is my new reality.

I walk inside to find my new notebook from Dr. Thorne, and write down; *I am sad for the loss of the person Dylan impersonated. His pretty exterior hid from me the truth that inside of him lived a monster.*

# EPILOGUE

It has been six months since Dylan died. For weeks after his funeral, I lived in a fog of despair. I was crippled by my emotional pain; riddled by depression, loneliness, sadness, and anger. I knew I had to get better for myself and my children, but couldn't see how. Once I accepted the truth, that Dylan died by my hands, I hated myself, even though I knew that he was a vile human being. Most days, I stayed home and hid from the outside world. During that time, prying myself from bed became part of my morning ritual. At night, insomnia was my constant companion. When I closed my eyes, I couldn't stop thinking about the what-ifs. What if I had taken the hidden key in from outside, so Dylan couldn't have come in that night? What if I had just ignored Dylan that night at Barnacles? Then he would never have come into my life. What if Dylan had just killed me? Then I wouldn't be in this horrible state.

Appointments with Dr. Thorne were and still are the high points for me every week. First, she encouraged me to stop the self-criticism. She wanted me to work towards forgiving myself. She called it "self-compassion." She said that for years, I have taken care of everyone's needs, but now it's time for me to take care of myself.

She suggested that I start meditating, but I couldn't be still for that long. I found that crocheting had some of the same benefits. Sitting silently for hours helps relax and comfort me. Kat is now calling me "Martha Stewart." I feel such gratification when I finish each project. I began with creating afghans and scarves, but now I'm producing a hat a day. Lauren gives them out to her friends at school. I love it whenever I get a text with a picture of them wearing their new hats.

Dr. Thorne has also helped me see that good things can come out of bad situations. We spoke of how sad I was when my marriage to John ended. I thought I had failed my children, my parents, and myself. Now I can see how Lauren and Jack have benefitted from the divorce. Not only do they get to celebrate two Christmas days every year, they have also been blessed with a loving stepmother and a new brother. But I have not found the upside of Dylan's death.

I miss Dylan's presence in my life. I'm still trying to deal with the fact that he hated me enough to try to kill me. I try to convince myself that I had the right to fight back, but now I wish I just had left him there on the floor and called the police. I remember being petrified that he would get up and kill me and my kids. Now, knowing that his neck was broken makes it harder to accept that I was right in killing him. If only I'd known that he wasn't a threat at that moment.

When I told Dr. Thorne about these conflicting feelings, she told me that I'd had a natural human reaction to being attacked. The fight-or-flight response is self-explanatory. Dr. Thorne said that since I couldn't run, I was forced to fight to survive.

I'm trying to learn from each of my immoral mistakes, and how not to repeat them. I'm taking a break from dating. The way my last relationship ended spares me any questions about my love life. It's empowering to just count on myself. There are still ugly rumors being spread about me, but when I hear them I tell myself, "I'm the only one who can control how I feel about my past. What others might think or say are of no concern to me." This mantra helps me drown out the gossip.

Throughout my life, I've used humor to mask my feelings about my heartbreaks. I still get big laughs when I say, "I've been married two times, but I'm sure the third will be a charm!" I've been told that I have an innate ability to laugh at myself. But the death of Dylan is no laughing matter. I asked Kat for a moratorium on making jokes about him. She has stayed true to her promise, now only making self-deprecating jokes.

My kids have been very supportive. Lauren has been training with me to run a 5K in April for mental health awareness. She's also been busy applying to all the Ivy League colleges. Thankfully, she's ridden out this storm rather well. Her grade point average has stayed at a 4.5. It's a reminder of why we needed to shield her from the truth. If she knew the bigger role she played in Dylan's death, she'd be devastated.

Jack's football season concluded with Tree Lawn High School being state champs. Cheering for him at those Friday night games felt electric. At first, I hated when the parent of a player was quick to hug me. It was hard to except their compassion for me, but towards the end of the season, I started to look forward to those hugs.

Kat has shown great resilience these past six months, and her friendship has been steadfast. She stood next to me at every one of Jack's games. She says that she's determined to nurse me back to health. She rarely makes fun of me anymore, but still makes me laugh. She has surprised me with her unbridled daily support. Every single morning, she calls and enthusiastically says, "Good morning, sunshine!" Who knew she had this maternal side?

Some nights, Kat likes to drag me to Tree Lawn's only bar and restaurant, The Varsity Club. She thinks that there's no better cure for a broken heart than a cold beer and a hot bartender. Our favorite bartender looks like an older version of Brad Pitt. Kat calls him "Jimmy Blue-Eyes." These happy times help me believe that I will be alright, and that life is good. She gets me to smile by telling me about all her daily antics. We're there so often, we're now part of a group the bartenders call "the regulars." This group of people comes from similar backgrounds, but are all different ages. I enjoy hearing about their days at work or on the golf course. They have never uttered a negative thing to me about my past. I'm trying to surround myself with only positive people.

Sometimes we see Tommy's dad, Pete, somber and bellied up to the bar. At first, I hadn't recognized him, because he's put on a lot of weight. He keeps to himself with his head low, drinking for hours. He'll wave to me from time to time, but we haven't spoken since Dylan died.

At the bar tonight, I feel exceptionally cheerful. I imagine it's from all the endorphins flowing through my veins from my long run this morning: proof that I'm getting back to my old self. As usual, Kat is holding court with the regulars. She's standing in front of the small crowd, telling one funny story after another. She has us all in hysterics. I see Pete at the end of the bar. He appears to be listening to Kat's stories. His demeanor makes me think that he's very drunk. He gets up from his stool and falls back, hitting the ground with a loud thump. Kat and I run over to assist him up. We each take a hand and pull him up off the floor. He looks and smells bad, like he's decaying. We get him back onto his stool, and he jerks his arms away.

Pete turns his head and looks right at me. "I'm really sorry."

"No worries," I assure him. "We've all had a few too many."

Kat and I start to walk back to our stools, when we hear Pete say, "I'm sorry for what I did."

Kat turns and loudly asks, "What did you do, Pete?"

"I'm sorry that I let Jen believe she did it."

Kat's face reddens. "What did you let Jen believe she did, Pete?"

A chill runs down my spine. Pushing Kat aside, I run to Pete and yell, "I didn't kill Dylan, did I?"

"No, you didn't." He pauses. "I did."

Kat leans into him and says under her breath, "You're fucking telling me that you killed Dylan that night?"

"Yes. McDonald told me that Dylan was still alive. I hated that asshole for what he did to Tommy. I wanted him dead. I just did it. I covered his mouth and pinched his nose until he was dead."

A giant wave of emotion pours out of me. I'm crying at first, then laughing uncontrollably. I find myself jumping up and down, throwing my arms up into the air.

Kat leans back and puts her hands over her face, making a high pitch noise. I think she's screaming. This stops me in my tracks, and I grab onto her, looking into her eyes. She's crying.

"Kat, I knew it!" I yell, "I knew I didn't kill him!"

She hugs me like a mother would after finding their lost child, as happy as I am to know the truth.

Pete interrupts, slurring, "I'm so sorry that I didn't tell you. The case was closed, and I thought I'd gotten away with it. But when I saw how hard you're taking all this, I knew that I was wrong."

Kat's excited mood switches to anger. "You fucking idiot! Do you know what my friend here has been through? All this time, you let her think that she killed Dylan?"

Pete waves his hands, trying to shield himself from Kat's shaming. I pull Kat away from his face, then stand close and place my hands on his shoulders. With tears of joy still running down my face, I whisper. "You've done a great thing here. You have freed my soul from despair. I'm not angry with you. I'm thankful that you found the courage to tell me what really happened that horrible night."

I turn to see Kat hugging everyone at the bar. I can feel my smile squeezing my face. I've been freed from my prison of guilt for Dylan's death.

With his head down, Pete starts to walk out of the bar. I remember that Dylan's neck had been broken by Lauren. I panic. Pete's confession cannot reopen the case. I run to him and grab him from behind, and whisper into his ear, "Pete, we don't have to tell anyone else the truth. It's over. I don't want to rehash it. Please, let's try to move forward. I forgive you, Pete, I really do."

He pats my hand on his shoulder and says, "Jen, I will do whatever you want me to do."

"Pete, I'm not innocent either. I did try to kill Dylan. Let's keep your confession between us. Go live your life."

His body shivers under my arms. He turns and gives me a long hug. "Thank you, Jen."

We step back from each other and make eye contact. He nods his head, then walks out the door. Feeling relief, I skip back to the regulars. One by one they take turns hugging me. I can see Jimmy Blue-Eyes watching me. He comes out from behind the bar, scoops me up, and gives me a twirl.

Still in his embrace, I grin at Kat and give her a wink.

Smiling, Kat utters, "Oh, here she goes again!"

Laughing, I lean away from Jimmy. "No way. No more pretty boys for me!"

Kat laughs. "Thank God for that!

Made in the USA
Lexington, KY
18 December 2017